Also by Julie B Cosgrove

Wordplay Mysteries

Word Has It
In Other Words (coming soon)

Relatively Seeking Mysteries

One Leaf Too Many
Fallen Leaf
Leaf Me Alone

Bunco Biddies Series

Dumpster Dicing
Baby Bunco
Threes, Sixes & Thieves
'Til Dice Do Us Part

WORD

GETS AROUND

by

JULIE B COSGROVE

P

Write Integrity Press, LLC

Word Gets Around
© 2021 Julie B Cosgrove

ISBN: 978-1-944120-97-9

Published by Pursued Books:
an imprint of Write Integrity Press, LLC
PO Box 702852
Dallas, TX 75370

Find out more about the author, Julie B Cosgrove, at her website: www.juliebcosgrove.com or on her author page at www.WriteIntegrity.com.

Printed in the United States of America.

DEDICATION

Dedicated to all who dare to write the truth,
   especially in this day when so many others spin lies.

I do not write to you because you do not know the truth, but because you do know it and because no lie comes from the truth. 1 John 2:21

Contents

CAST OF CHARACTERS

Wanda Lee Warner – A widow who loves word games. She has lived in Scrub Oak, TX, most of her life. She has a natural curiosity about events in her town because she loves her community and its residents. She has a dachshund named Sophie.

Betty Sue Simpson – Wanda's best friend since they were kids. She is also a widow. As a retired elementary school teacher, she knows the background of almost everyone who has lived in town since 1965. She also likes word games and puzzles.

Evelyn Joseph – Wanda's next-door neighbor who moved to Scrub Oak ten years ago to care for her sister until she passed from cancer. The widow of an Army Intelligence officer, who was killed in the Gulf War in 1990, she never remarried. She stayed in Scrub Oak because she and Wanda became good friends and she wanted to finally put down roots.

Todd Martin – Wanda's nephew, who has returned to Scrub Oak to join the police force. They have always been close and enjoy a good game of Scrabble together on Thursday mornings before his shift. He lived with Wanda during his high school years after his parents divorced.

Hazel Perks – A neighbor who lives near the old, abandoned Ferguson Mansion and is an avid gardener, which also keeps her aware of the goings on in her neighborhood. She grows prize roses.

Debi Castro – Once a star student in Scrub Oak, after getting her journalism degree, she returned to write for *The Oakmont County Weekly Gazette*, as well as other online papers in Texas.

Mayor Arnold Porter – Has been the mayor of Scrub Oak for over twenty years. He is rather pompous about his power, but deep down has the community's best interests at heart.

Chief Brooks – The police chief of Scrub Oak. All business and a stickler for rules, but underneath he has a soft heart.

Pastor Bob Thomas – The clergyman at Holy Hill Church where Wanda attends.

Fred Ballinger – The retired principal of Scrub Oak's lower school. He has eyes for Betty Sue.

Priscilla Tucker – Owner of the Coffee Bean, a local coffee shop that sells organic roasts from all over the world. Her sister, Sally, runs Sally's Salads which also features the organic blends.

Ray O'Malley – Owner of the Hook & Owl Irish Pub, which also makes great Irish Stew, Evelyn's favorite.

Sally Ibson – Owner of Sally's Salads, but she also serves breakfast breads and coffee from her sister's Coffee Bean.

Barbara Mills – The librarian, who is also secretary for the City Council and local Audubon Society.

Tom Jacobs – Owner of Tom's Thrift Shop and local editor for the *Oakmont County Weekly Gazette*. His wife is **Misty Jacobs.** His grown daughter is **Vicki Jacobs.**

Mason Clyburn – Vicki's fiancé. A business major who is going for a second degree in journalism. He helps out at *The Oakmont County Weekly Gazette.*

Ben Bolton – Owner of the Big B BBQ near the Woodway Resort. A gentle giant who used to play linebacker for the Dallas Cowboys back in the day, he owns Better Burgers, that his son **Keith Bolton**, Debi's fiancé, runs.

Mary Lou Fitzgerald – A new mother with a baby named Lucy who is the organist at Holy Hill Church and was a high school teacher.

Zelda Lewis – Runs Zelda's Zumba and she also teaches Pilates as well as other exercise and dance classes. She sells herbs and essential oils on the side. Her husband, Vlad, is a carpenter.

Collin and Claudia Rollins – Runs A Cut Above, a barber/beauty salon that plays only contemporary Christian songs. Collin is a neighborhood watch captain.

Frank Patterson – A nice old guy with COPD from years of smoking foul-smelling stogies. Now he sucks on thick pretzel sticks and always has one in his mouth. He lives behind Wanda. Quiet, but his eyes see a lot that goes on.

Finn and Emma Mae Buckley – Live across from Frank. She is the receptionist at Schiller and Smith. Finn, an extraordinary handyman, works odd jobs around town. Everyone calls him Fix-it Finn.

Melissa Suntych – An artist who lives on the edge of town off Woodway Drive and rescues animals, domestic and wild. She and her husband, Jerry, are on the neighborhood watch.

Scrub Oak Texas

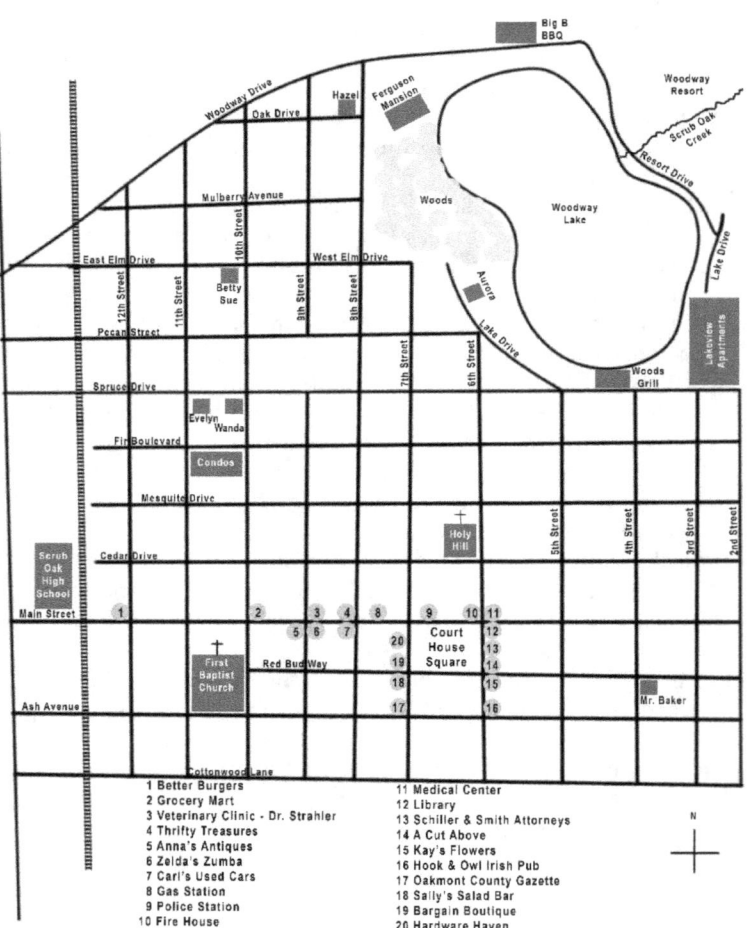

1 Better Burgers
2 Grocery Mart
3 Veterinary Clinic - Dr. Strahler
4 Thrifty Treasures
5 Anna's Antiques
6 Zelda's Zumba
7 Carl's Used Cars
8 Gas Station
9 Police Station
10 Fire House

11 Medical Center
12 Library
13 Schiller & Smith Attorneys
14 A Cut Above
15 Kay's Flowers
16 Hook & Owl Irish Pub
17 Oakmont County Gazette
18 Sally's Salad Bar
19 Bargain Boutique
20 Hardware Haven

CHAPTER ONE

It had been three months since Wanda Lee Turner had dared to open the box. She'd stuffed it into the top shelf of her bedroom closet. Didn't matter. She knew it lurked there.

Sometimes, in the middle of the night, she'd roll over in bed, stare at the closed door, and envision it, beckoning her to lift the lid and begin the mystery.

"You're overreacting, Aunt Wanda." Todd Martin peered at her over his mug of coffee. He sat at her kitchen table the way he always did on Thursday mornings, his day off as a patrol officer for the Scrub Oak Police Department. "It's been weeks, no months, since the Scrabble board held clues to solving the murders at the Ferguson Mansion."

"I know. And I used to love playing the word game with you."

"You used to love playing it with anyone who walked through the door." He reached for the creamer. "This stuff is awful. Another one of Priscilla's latest and greatest blends?"

"It is. Ugandan Supreme. I think that's the name."

"Thought so. I could smell it before I opened the door."

"That bad, huh?" She plopped down across from him and took a sip of the new flavor featured at the Coffee Bean. She had hated to disappoint Priscilla Tucker, who ran the bistro inside the Grocery Mart. So, she'd bought a bag. Like most of the selections, it tasted too strong, too bitter, and too pungent.

The java roast assaulted her taste buds, sending a shiver through her torso. "Ugh. You're right. This wins the prize for the nastiest one yet."

Wanda grabbed his mug. She dumped its contents into the sink along with hers. She rinsed out the dispenser and waved goodbye to the grounds swirling down the disposal drain. Then she plopped some good old-fashioned, lighter-blend American coffee pods in the brewer. Within a few seconds she returned the mugs to the table. "There. Less of a hassle anyway."

Todd kissed her cheek. "Thanks, Aunt Wanda. Now where is the box?"

"Not tellin'." She pouted with her arms crossed like a three-year-old.

Todd laughed, which made her chuckle as well. "You need professional help, you know."

"I do not." She swatted at him playfully. Then her mood become solemn. "I simply don't want another incident. Seeing those clues spelled out ahead of time still makes my skin all goose bumpety."

He lifted a finger. "Isolated incident. Happened one time out of how many hundreds of games we have played over the years? God works in mysterious ways, but how many of those unique occurrences appear more than once in the Bible, huh?"

"True." Wanda rubbed her temple. "Okay. Next Thursday we will play a game. Promise."

"Good." Todd rose with a wink and set his buff-colored Stetson on his head. It always made him appear so grown up, so authoritative. "See ya."

Wanda glanced at the clock on her kitchen wall. Only ten after ten? "What's the hurry?"

He stopped with his hand on the backdoor knob. "Got a ton of laundry to do and my apartment is a pig sty."

Before she could reply, he left.

Wanda leaned back and grinned. In her recollection, the only time a single guy did housekeeping was when he had a date. Good. He needed more of a social life. Maybe he'd met someone where he lived. The Lake View Apartments catered to young professionals who wished to escape their hectic business lives in nearby Fort Worth for some well-needed peace and quiet.

Some of the residents had poo-pooed the development, but Wanda welcomed it. Too many small North Texas towns were shriveling up quicker than the skin on their long-term residents. Towns needed youthfulness to adapt and survive. And truth be told, several of the long-term residents were thankful when young urban families wanted to buy and renovate their homesteads so they could move into the urban assisted living centers nearer to the big city medical facilities. The circle of life.

Speaking of which, she and Betty Sue were to go visit Old Mrs. Tucker in one of those centers today. Yipes, she had totally forgotten. Where was her brain?

"Do you know where I laid it this morning, Sophie?" Wanda bent to scratch the velvety floppy ears of her dachshund as she lay in her doggie bed by the refrigerator. Soulful, brown eyes gazed back, and a slightly curved, thin tail wiggled in a small wag.

Wanda patted the pooch's head and walked down the hallway to her bedroom. Fifteen minutes later she locked the backdoor, something she never did before the robberies and double-murder three months ago. As chairperson of the newly organized neighborhood crime watch, she felt an obligation to set a good example.

She walked to her car which was parked in the driveway. A folded piece of white paper perched under her windshield wiper on the driver's side. What, an advertisement? Who would spend money for that in this small town?

As Wanda removed it, she noticed it had light blue lines on it. School notebook paper. Weird. She unfolded it and read the note. It contained one word only, printed neatly in large letters with a thick black marker. *Better.*

What on earth?

"See you got one as well."

Wanda swung around at the sound of her best friend, Betty Sue Simpson's voice. She'd walked the two blocks between their homes to meet Wanda. Betty Sue made a habit of walking around town instead of driving to keep the recently lost forty pounds from finding her hips again.

She waved a similar piece of paper. "At first I thought it came from one of my former students. But I've been retired a while."

"What does yours say?" Wanda held her one-word message up for her friend to read.

Betty Sue halted as she unfolded her note. As she did, Wanda detected the pattern identical to the way hers had been folded. Over twice and then in thirds. Had to be from the same source.

The word on Betty Sue's appeared to be in the same penmanship. *Report.*

"I don't get it. Report what?" Betty Sue shook her head, her soft curls bouncing in late morning sunlight.

"Beats me." Wanda folded hers and placed it in her purse. Then she clicked the fob twice to open her car doors.

"Maybe more people around town have gotten these and if we put them all together it will make sense."

"Ah, a scavenger hunt with words. I like that." Wanda grinned. She'd always loved word games. "I wonder who is doing this?"

"Who knows? But if I were a betting woman, I'd say we will find out soon enough. It'll be the talk of the town by evening." Betty Sue opened the passenger door and slid into the front seat.

"True." Perhaps she'd learn more tonight at the weekly neighborhood watch captains' meeting.

As the two drove to visit Mrs. Tucker, Wanda couldn't help but think that Scrabble board of hers would once again hold the answer.

But did she want to find out?

CHAPTER TWO

Wanda tapped the steering wheel as they traveled down the rural highway.

"Your brain is whirling, I can tell."

"You know me too well, Betty Sue. At times that is comforting, at other times, not so much."

Her friend's melodious giggle filled the car. They'd known each other since elementary school. They were more like sisters, except they rarely argued or showed their claws as sisters often do. Not really.

"Yes, you're right. I've been thinking. Why would someone send us notes like that?"

"Maybe this is a new social game people are playing and somebody has started it in Scrub Oak." Betty Sue refolded hers and put it inside her purse.

"It is sort of a fun idea. Perhaps we will all get invites to bring our words and put them together. A social gathering. But who would do this?"

"Maybe Sally did, in an effort to get more people to

come eat soups and salads?" Betty Sue shrugged. "Or Priscilla, so she can promote her new coffee blend."

Wanda stuck out her tongue. "Tried it. Yuck."

"Good to know."

Wanda rolled her eyes. "Or Zelda, to get more people to take Zumba lessons?"

"You were going to start coming with me on Monday and Wednesday mornings." Betty Sue flashed her a teacher's arched eyebrow.

Wanda waggled her head as she slowed to turn the corner onto the road that led to the assisted living center. "Yeah, I know. I should. Stop nagging."

Betty Sue opened her mouth but shut it again. She chuckled and turned to gaze out the side window onto the fields dotted with mesquite and scrub oaks. A doe and two fawns grazed under one. As they passed by, the trio lifted their heads and froze in place.

"Aw. How precious. Thank goodness they have a few more months to grow before hunting season erupts." In Texas, it didn't get cool enough to go deer hunting until November.

"Don't remind me." Wanda sighed through her nose. The previous fall, a hunting accident had turned into a murder investigation, thanks to Wanda and the Scrabble board clues.

Betty Sue turned the knob on the air conditioner. "I know September is one of the hottest months here, but I always think it should be cooler by now. Guess too many years of hanging fall leaves on Welcome Back to School bulletin boards has tainted me."

"Yep. How these kids play football in ninety-degree weather with all that padding on is beyond me. But they do."

Betty Sue swiveled to meet her friend's eyes. "Of course, they do. Friday night fever is alive and well, my dear. If it ever stops, this state will wither and die."

The two laughed as they turned into the gates.

Mrs. Tucker wasn't feeling well that day. She would not be seeing visitors after all, the nurse whispered to them as they stood in the foyer. But there was a Scrabble tournament in the parlor if Betty Sue and Wanda wanted to join in.

Betty Sue glanced at Wanda to give the answer.

Wanda shook her head. "Not today. Thank you, though."

Betty Sue hissed at her as they pushed open the double doors that led to the porte cochere. "I don't get you. Three months ago, you'd jump at the chance to spend the morning playing word games."

Wanda stopped and stared at the wisteria letting loose their last blooms, coating the grounds like confetti after a parade. "I know. Todd is right. I need help."

Betty Sue hooked her hand through Wanda's elbow. "What you need is a nice evening with friends. I am inviting Evelyn and Hazel over and we will have a potluck and play Scrabble."

"But, what if . . .?"

"Wanda, nothing sinister will happen. You'll have fun and it'll put the gleam back in your eyes. It has been missing, you know."

Wanda turned and gazed at her reflection in the beveled glass inserts of the entrance door. "It has?" She straightened her back. "I guess the responsibility of chairing the neighborhood watches had been more taxing on me than I realized."

"Well, people have been more antsy after those robbers were running loose. And to think one of our own might have been a murderer? That burst the small-town security bubble of everyone knowing everybody."

"True. But the words in the Scrabble game Todd and I played gave us clues that led us to the culprits. What if it does something similar again?" A sudden trepidation gripped Wanda in the chest.

"Then it needs solving." Betty Sue patted Wanda's arm, her favorite gesture to assure or calm someone. "Now never you mind. There hasn't been any crime in this area all summer. You have the respect of the community in forming these watches. Our town is safe again, partially because of your tenacity."

"Oh, pooh." She swatted away the compliment.

A humbled pride swelled over the trepidation like an ocean wave over the sand, dragging away any doubts as it receded. "Okay, we'll get together and play a game or two. But for now, let's stop off at the Woods Grill and treat ourselves to a blackened chicken cobb salad. How about that?"

Betty Sue side-hugged her. "Now you're talking."

As they entered the parking lot, Wanda received a text from Evelyn, her next-door neighbor. *Found this on my windshield. Any clue?*

A photo, obviously taken with her phone, followed. An unfolded piece of notebook paper revealed the word *Before* printed with thick black marker strokes.

Wanda turned to Betty Sue, whose mouth had opened wide enough to catch one of the Scrub Oak football team's passes.

"I just lost my appetite. You?"

Betty Sue gulped and nodded.

Wanda tapped over the qwerty board on her phone. *Got similar. Betty Sue ditto. Meet us at my place in a half hour.*

"We have a new mystery brewing, don't we?" Betty Sue bit the bottom side of her lip.

Wanda's hand trembled as she pocketed her phone and dug out her car keys. "Exactly. Let's go."

Julie B Cosgrove

CHAPTER THREE

Wanda stared at the three pieces of paper unfolded on her kitchen table. Betty Sue and Evelyn hovered near by.

"Well?" Evelyn glanced at both of her friends. "Whatcha think?"

Wanda blew out a long breath. "I haven't a clue. *Better Report Before* . . . what?"

"It could be *Before Report Better.*" Betty Sue rearranged the papers. "Um, nah. That doesn't make any sense."

"Wait here." Wanda dashed down the hall, opened her closet door, and grabbed the Scrabble box with her fingertips, wobbling on tiptoe. She caught it as it toppled into her hands and brought it to her chest like hugging an old friend. The aroma of the cardboard, the slight whiff of the wooden tiles and tile holders, and the muffled rattle of the letters in the bag awakened her senses.

A feeling of purpose and rejuvenation settled over her as she returned to the kitchen. She didn't believe in Ouija boards or palm reading, but Todd's point had been valid. God worked in mysterious ways. Pastor Bob of Holy Hill Church had sermonized on the various ways God speaks to those who have the faith to listen with their souls. Nature scenes, Bible verses, hymn lyrics, and everyday activities had all been inspirations in his life. Who was to say the Holy Spirit couldn't speak through a word game, the activity she'd loved all her life? Had He not several months before?

She set the box on the counter, opened it, and unfolded the board.

Betty Sue grinned at her as she picked up the three pieces of paper. "What are you thinking?"

"All three words have the letters *r* and *e* in common. *Better* and *report* have *t* in them. *Before* and *report* have *o*. *Better* and *before* have *b*. Maybe if we laid them out on the Scrabble board it will mean something."

She dumped the letter tiles onto the countertop and began to find the ones to spell out the three words. As she did, Evelyn transferred them to the game board. She started with the star in the center of the board and placed the letters for *better*. Then she built off the *b* and spelled the word *before*. Lastly, she played off the *r* in *better* and laid down the tiles to make the word *report*.

"They each have six letters." Betty Sue pointed to the words Evelyn placed on the squares.

Evelyn's eyes widened as she backed up two paces. "Three sixes? That's not good."

Wanda patted her arm. "Let's not assume it to be evil

just yet."

Betty Sue angled her head as she studied the pattern. "Hmm. If we had a six-letter word that started with an *e* and ended in a *t* we'd make a box."

"*Expert* works." Wanda sat down at the table. The other two did the same.

"As do *effort* and *export*."

"True, Betty Sue." Wanda leaned back and rubbed an eyebrow. "But we don't have any of those words."

Evelyn groaned.

Wanda turned to her. "What is it, Ev?"

"It's true. We don't have more words." She swallowed. "Not yet."

Julie B Cosgrove

CHAPTER FOUR

The phone rang. Wanda gazed at the caller ID on her screen and mouthed the name "Hazel." Widowed like Wanda, Betty Sue, and Evelyn, Hazel lived on 8th across the street from the edge of the woods that backed up to the lake and the Ferguson Mansion, the site of one of the recent murders.

"Hi, Hazel. What's up?"

"I got this weird note."

Wanda felt the blood leave her face and she backstepped to a kitchen chair to sit down. "I see."

Betty Sue and Evelyn both flashed her quizzical expressions.

Wanda gazed back at them as she responded. "We all got the same thing. What word is on yours?"

The other two sucked in a deep breath.

"It's *expert*. I know it." Evelyn tapped her fingernail onto the board.

"I bet it's *effort*. Better report effort before . . ."

"Before what?" Evelyn shrugged.

Wanda pulled the phone from her ear. "Stop."

"Okay." Betty Sue's mouth pressed shut.

"Excuse us for interrupting." Evelyn jerked her head back a bit, her eyebrows almost meeting in the center.

Wanda lowered her voice to a whisper. "No. That's her word. Stop."

The two responded together. "Oh."

"That doesn't start with an *e*." Evelyn gave her head a sharp shake. "Nor does it have an *r* or a *b*."

Wanda rose and walked back to the counter to dig through the tiles. "Hazel, we all received similar notes. Can you bring yours over now?"

Hazel replied that she was on the way.

"Good. We're in the kitchen. Come around back." In Scrub Oak, very few people used the front door unless they were selling something. Except young men picking up their dates, of course.

"Where does that word fit?"

"Here, Ev." Wanda brought the letters *p, o* and *s* over then placed them around the second *t* in the word *better*.

"That doesn't make anything." Evelyn scrunched her nose. "I was hoping for a square. At least that would make sense and if there were more letters, they would fill in the center."

"This isn't a crossword puzzle. You never know the pattern a Scrabble game will take. That's part of the fun." Wanda smiled.

She had to admit seeing the board on her kitchen table again felt normal. She and Todd had played Scrabble since he was in third grade. When he left for college, he had gifted her his dictionary. He'd written inside the flap, "We will always have words between us."

And so, they had, every Thursday morning since he returned to Scrub Oak after graduating from college with a degree in criminal science and then from the police academy with the rank of sergeant. That is until three months ago . . .

Betty Sue waved her hands. "Maybe it's all about the squares the letters land on. That's the purpose of the game, right? Score the highest points."

"Well then, *stop* ends on the triple letter spot." Wanda counted the points. "That makes twelve points."

"Twelve months in the year. Twelve disciples." Evelyn sighed. "Neither of those make sense."

"Good try, though. Let's add up the others." Wanda got out the score pad and began to count the points. "*Report* lands on a double word score so that adds up to sixteen."

"Eighteen." Betty Sue shifted the first *e* to reveal a double letter square.

"Good catch." Wanda felt the blood rush back into her cheeks. She should have seen that. She truly had become rusty. "Both the words *better* and *before* start on the star, so either one could also be a double score."

"You handed me the letters for *better* first." Evelyn counted. "So that would be sixteen points."

"Okay, then the word *before* adds up to twelve."

Betty Sue wrote the numbers down on a scorepad. "Twelve, eighteen, sixteen, and twelve. Mean anything?"

"Nope." Wanda and Evelyn responded together.

Wanda pushed away from the table "This is nonsense."

"Maybe there will be something different about Hazel's word and that will solve this dilemma."

"True, Ev. After all, we haven't actually seen it."

"Here she is now." Betty Sue rose to let her in as she tapped on the backdoor.

Hazel dug the note out of her pocket and opened it. Folded the same way as the others and on the same type of lined notebook paper, she laid it on the table next to theirs. "What does this all mean?"

Wanda shook her head. "We have no idea. But I have a feeling we are not the only ones who got these on their windshields today. All we can do is wait and see how many others surface."

She lifted the board and placed it on top of the refrigerator, then placed the tile bag and holders there as well.

"Now, who wants a chicken salad sandwich?"

Evelyn and Hazel raised their hands.

Betty Sue didn't.

"It's not that fattening. I use an avocado mayo I make myself. You told me they contained good fats. Besides, a tablespoon is only eight calories."

"It's not that. I love your chicken salad." Betty Sue

massaged her midsection. "It's only that I have an eerie feeling in my gut that these notes were placed on our specific cars for a reason, which means two things."

"And those are?" Wanda lifted the Saran-wrapped bowl from the fridge along with a head of Boston lettuce.

Betty Sue held up a finger. "First, they knew where we lived and what cars we drive."

"Well, it is Scrub Oak, dear." Evelyn folded her hands. "It's not as if we lived in a metropolis where no one knows their neighbors."

"True." Hazel glanced back and forth between them.

Wanda retrieved a spreading spatula. "What's the second thing, Betty Sue?"

"Well, Wanda it occurs to me we were chosen to receive these for a reason. After all, it was the four of us who helped solve the last crime."

Wanda felt a shiver wiggle up her spine. "So?"

"So, maybe you need to tell Todd."

"Betty Sue, what would I tell him? We got cryptic notes on our cars. Could be a kid's prank."

The other two ladies mumbled in agreement. Betty Sue shrugged and placed her chin in her hands, studying the board again.

"No, we need to wait. If I learned anything from the last time it was that. Wait and let the evidence reveal itself." Wanda turned her back to her friends and began slapping the chicken salad on slices of seven-grain bread.

Silence settled around the kitchen. Wanda figured

every one of them thought the same thing. When would the next word appear and where? And what would it be?

Avocado Mayonnaise

Ingredients

- One mashed ripe, black-skinned avocado
- 2 teaspoons white or cider vinegar
- 2 teaspoons lemon juice, fresh is best
- ¾ teaspoon onion powder
- ¼ teaspoon salt
- ¼ cup water
- 2 tablespoons avocado oil

Instructions

1. Scoop out the green "meat" from the avocado and discard the seed. Mash with a fork.
2. Combine all ingredients in a blender until smooth.
3. Add more water if a thinner mayo spread is desired.
4. If you want a spicy mayo, feel free to add a dash of hot sauce or cayenne pepper.
5. Store leftovers covered in the fridge for no longer than 3-4 days.

CHAPTER FIVE

Ten minutes later, Pricilla phoned Wanda.

"This may sound weird, but I went out to my car a few minutes ago. I'd left my phone in it all morning. The early-rising coffee crowd was thicker than usual. In fact, I've ordered more boxes of that new Ugandan brew. It is selling like mad."

"Really?" Wanda wondered who would buy the stuff.

"Yes. One of my best sellers so far. Anyway, I realized I'd left my phone in the car. By the time I cleaned up, the late morning coffee crowd filtered in, no pun intended."

Wanda chuckled. "Okay?"

"Once things quieted down, I glanced at the wall clock, and it was half past eleven. When I went a few minutes ago to get my phone there was a weird note tucked under the windshield wipers."

Wanda glanced at her friends. She cupped her hand over the phone. "It's Priscilla. She's gotten one, too."

The others immediately began murmuring. Wanda

shushed them with her hand and put the call on speaker phone. "Let me guess. One word written in large letters on a piece of notebook paper."

Priscilla let out a gasp. "Well, yes, as a matter of fact. How did you know?"

"Betty Sue, Hazel, Evelyn, and I all received one today. What does yours say?"

"Debi."

Wanda edged over to the counter and began sorting through the letter tiles. "As in D...E...B...B...I...E? A girl's name?"

"No, with one *b*. And it ends in an *i*."

Betty Sue perked up. "Does she mean Debi Castro? One of the best students to come through Scrub Oak Independent School District. She won prizes for her writing and recently won the Charles E. Green statewide award for reporting excellence. Quite a shining star."

"Wow." Evelyn whistled. "How come she is with *The Gazette* instead of a big city paper?"

Wanda tapped her temple. "I recall Todd telling me why. She agreed to the position because she'd become engaged to one of Ben Bolton's sons, Keith. They all went to school together."

Betty Sue nodded. "But she's landed several exposés for the *Dallas Morning News* and *Austin American Statesman* online."

"Ever since Tom hired Debi Castro as a reporter, the paper really has improved." Hazel eyed the board as Wanda set the letters in the reporter's name down on it.

"So that's why Ben let Keith take over running Better Burgers while he and Les handled Big B BBQ." Betty Sue smiled. "To give the boy a future."

"I guess. But the letters in *Debi* don't fit anywhere on the board. There are only two *b* tiles in Scrabble." Wanda sat back down.

Evelyn began to shuffle the tiles around. "If you use the same *b* for *better* and *before*, then you have a *b* left over for *Debi*."

"Ah. Very good." Wanda gave her a high five.

A small, far away voice interrupted their reverie. "Are you all playing Scrabble?"

Then Wanda remembered she'd laid the phone down and Priscilla still waited on the other end. "Sort of. When did you get yours?"

"I have no idea. I arrived at six. So sometime between then and now."

"That's okay. Hey? Can you swing by after you close the Coffee Bean and bring that note over here? I want to show it to the neighborhood watch captains at the meeting tonight."

"Okay. I sure don't want it. See ya a little after six then." She hung up.

Evelyn rested her chin in her hand. "*Debi* might fit with the *e* in *better* or *report* if you used a blank tile for the *b*."

"Nope." Hazel raised a bony finger with a bit of dirt under the nail. No doubt she had been weeding around her prize roses today. "*Debi* is a proper noun. That's not allowed in Scrabble."

"Oh, for heaven's sake." Evelyn huffed a long sigh. "Maybe whoever is doing this doesn't know the rules."

"Then they wouldn't use a Scrabble board." Wanda placed the tiles anyway. "*Better report before Debi stop.* Stop what?"

Betty Sue crossed her arms over her chest. "Well, their grammar is atrocious. It would be *stops*, not *stop*. That means it can't be anyone local."

"Why?" The other three women asked in unison.

"Simple. We always emphasized grammar in Scrub Oak schools. None of my former students would make such a blunder." She sniffed for emphasis.

The four pair of eyes studied the board for a few minutes without saying another word.

After a while, Evelyn groaned. "My eyes are crossing."

"Hey. That's it. Maybe this is supposed to be a crossword puzzle." Hazel's eyes sparkled.

"We ruled that out before you came over." Evelyn nodded at Wanda.

"Because?" Hazel glanced at each one.

"Crossword puzzles always have clues." Betty Sue bobbed her head once in affirmation. "Where are the clues?"

"Right, and there are no directions, up or down." Evelyn stacked the notebook papers together.

"Well, then there aren't any clues that say what should

be placed on a double word or triple letter score." Hazel's lip drooped a bit. "Why do you think it's Scrabble?"

Wanda raised her hands. "Ladies. We are getting off track. I suggest we all go home and ponder this. I'll poll the captains tonight to see if anyone else in their neighborhoods have gotten these today. We may only be scratching the surface."

Betty Sue straightened in her chair. "Wanda's right. These may not even go together. Until we have all the notes, we won't be able to come up with the true message."

Wanda rubbed her temple, which she often did when her brain was overtaxed. "And even then, we won't know who or why. I just pray this is not leading to another murder."

"Surely not in Scrub Oak." Hazel grabbed her purse and rose to leave.

Betty Sue let out a nervous giggle. "Three months ago, the idea of a murder in our town would have seemed absurd. But now?"

Exactly.

Julie B Cosgrove

CHAPTER SIX

A cardinal chirped outside the window, and the mantle clock's ticks echoed down the hall from the living room. Peace and quiet. Except after this morning's event, Wanda's mind was anything but that.

The notebook paper words rattled around in her brain. *Before, better, report, stop, Debi.* Were all of them that received these cryptic notes to work together to stop her? From what? Reporting better? Why?

Debi was a well-known, award-winning reporter. Her article about the enormous pressure on Texas high schools to graduate a large percentage of top-grade students had been eye-opening, not to mention, very well-written. No wonder she won that journalistic award.

Maybe someone at *The Gazette* was jealous because the county newspaper had also won awards since she came on board last year. In fact, it was planning to go digital, though most residents still enjoyed picking up the weekly copy at the grocery and convenience stores. But jealousy didn't make sense. It's not like this was Dallas or Houston with many reporters scrambling for the spotlight.

The Oakmont County Weekly Gazette only had three other workers that she knew of—Tom, the owner who also owned the thrift shop; Tom's daughter, Vicki, who acted as the receptionist; and Vicki's fiancé, Mason Clyburn, who helped with the graphics, layout, and editing. He had met Vicki through mutual friends at Baylor where he graduated with a degree in business management. This semester he attended Texas Christian University to earn a second degree in journalism. Obviously, the guy wanted to take over the Jacob's family businesses one day. Smart lad.

Oh, pooh. None of this added up. There had to be more messages yet to be discovered. She shoved the conundrum back into the recesses of her mind and occupied herself with other things, like sorting and doing her laundry.

A piercing ring echoed from down the hall. Wanda jolted. What was that sound coming from her bedroom?

Then her brain registered the source of the noise. Her landline. Few people called it anymore. In fact, she wondered why she paid for the thing every month. She answered the unit perched on her bedside table as she clutched the small cross dangling on her necklace with the other hand. "Hello?"

"It's Frank." A series of gurgled coughs interrupted his sentence. Frank, who lived behind Wanda, had COPD after decades of smoking foul-smelling stogies. Now he sucked on pretzel sticks and lectured the teenagers in town to never get hooked on tobacco.

Wanda waited for the episode to settle and her neighbor to clear his throat. Frank never called to chit-chat, so something had to be on his mind.

"Went out to the car. Strangest thing." He stopped to clear his throat once more.

An icy sensation splashed over Wanda's body once again. This time, it didn't feel quite as chilly. Maybe she was getting used to it. "Let me guess. A cryptic one-word message on notebook paper."

"Well, yes. Howdja . . .?"

"Seems several of us have gotten them. What does yours say?"

"*Nine.*"

"As in the number after eight?"

"Of course. I don't mean *no* in German for heaven's sake. Why? What numbers did you get?"

Wanda sat on the bed and fiddled with the ribbing on her throw pillow. "We didn't. We got other words. Is yours spelled out or is it the numeral?"

"Spelled out."

"May I come over and get it?"

"Why don't I bring it to you. I was about to head out to the pharmacy. That's why I went to my car in the first place."

"Okay, Frank. I'll be waiting out front at the curb. That way you can drive around and not get out."

She hung up and walked to her front yard to wait for

him. Within a few minutes the familiar light blue Buick rounded the corner and pulled up to her sidewalk. He waved the notebook paper at her as he lowered his car window.

Wanda bent to take it from his fingers. "Thanks, Frank." A blast of his AC hit her eyes as her ears detected Frank Sinatra crooning on his car radio. His mother's favorite singer, and thus his namesake.

"Another mystery to solve, eh?" He winked.

"It's looking that way."

Frank clucked his tongue. "Todd won't be happy." Then he waved and drove off.

Wanda whispered to herself as she watched him head down the street. "I know." Which, she reasoned, was exactly why she was not going to mention it to him. Not yet.

She walked back inside, placed the paper on the kitchen table, and spread out the others. Identical handwriting and black marker. What in the world?

She couldn't tell if the handwriting resembled a man's or a woman's. Too indistinct. Yet each was carefully penned. The pressure had been even. She could tell by the ink flow.

"Someone took their time, Sophie."

One floppy brown ear perked, then settled again. Soft snores resumed. Lucky dog.

Wanda bent down to pat her. "This is calculated. Planned. Someone thinks this is important. So why play games? Why not send *The Gazette* the entire message?"

A soft sigh was the only reply. A happy, thanks-for-loving-me sigh. The rest of the dachshund remained still, except for the tail.

Wanda laughed. "Are you sending me signals? Like in the Boy Scouts. Okay. I get the message. Treat?"

The dog's ears perked at the word. She stepped out of her basket and stood at attention near the pantry door.

As Wanda opened the box of dog biscuits her eye caught the Scrabble board where she'd placed it on top of the fridge. Darn that thing.

Sophie took her tasty treat to her bed in the corner. Wanda took the game from the fridge top and set it back on the kitchen table.

She picked out the tiles to spell the word *nine*.

It didn't fit right. That meant the message wasn't right.

"Of course." She spoke out loud and slapped her forehead.

Sophie stopped eating and cocked her head, the rest of the biscuit pressed in her paws.

Wanda phoned Evelyn. "Frank got one, too."

"What did his say?"

"*Nine*, as in the number." Wanda swallowed to control her breath as the tension rose in her chest.

"And?"

"We assumed the words were in the order when found them. But if they were all placed on our cars around the same time, well . . . the order could be different."

"Okay. I can see that."

"So, it could read, *Better Stop Debi Report Before*

Nine."

"Wouldn't that be Debi's with an apostrophe 's'?"

"Maybe, Ev. How about Debi better stop report before nine."

"That works, but . . ." Evelyn remained silent. Wanda at first thought perhaps they had been disconnected. Then her voice came through again, unusually soft for Evelyn.

"Didn't Betty Sue say she found her note about nine this morning?"

"Well, yes. And most likely that is around the time when ours could have been placed, even though a few of us found them later." Wanda sat down and stared at the board. "But if the notes were placed about nine, then . . .?"

"Debi has to stop the report before nine tonight. I wonder when *The Gazette* goes to print. It always comes out on Fridays, right?"

Wanda grinned. "Good thinking. I'll call Tom and ask."

He answered on the third ring. "Oakmont County Weekly Gazette."

"Tom. Wanda Warner. What time does the paper go to print tonight?"

"Nine o'clock. Why? You have something you want to add about the captains' meeting tonight? You could swing by after it's over, and I could put it in at the last minute."

"Yes, that would be wonderful. Thanks, Tom." Something told her not to reveal the cryptic notes to him at this point. She needed more evidence. Something concrete.

His voice came through her speaker again. "Better yet, why don't I come, take some notes, and then write up an article. I should attend these things on a regular basis, anyway, don't you think?"

"I agree. It helps to keep the town informed and promotes our efforts. Thanks, Tom. See ya tonight."

She redialed Evelyn's phone. "You were correct. It's nine o'clock tonight."

"So whatever report Debi is working on, someone doesn't want it to go to press."

"I don't have her number. I know she lives at the Lake View Apartments where Todd lives, though."

"Let's go grab a burger. Maybe she will be there seeing Keith, or he can give it to us."

That's what Wanda liked about Ev. She had an insatiable appetite but never gained a pound. She also was a practical-minded person. "Okay."

"We could ride around town and see if anyone else has a note on their windshield. Perhaps someone has not used their car today. Then we might learn what report."

"I suppose. Are you driving, or am I?"

"I will. That way you can keep your eyes peeled. My cataracts are getting worse."

Wanda sucked in a breath. She refrained from chiding her friend about not making an eye appointment. "Very well. Meet ya outside in a few."

Just as she tucked her phone in her purse it rang. Betty Sue.

"Hey. What's up?"

Her voice sounded labored and a tad shaky. "I'm here at Better Burgers. Yes, I know. I am breaking my diet. Anyway, Keith is all a tither. It seems Debi never showed up for lunch at one. They were to go over the wording on the wedding invitations. She is not answering her phone, and get this ..."

"No one at *The Gazette* has seen her today either?"

"Howdja know?"

Wanda slumped to the chair. The clock in the living room chimed five. "We weren't fast enough."

CHAPTER SEVEN

Wanda barely heard Betty Sue ask her what she meant. Her mind swirled with the what-ifs. Why had they assumed they'd discovered the words in the order they were meant to be in?

Whoever dropped them off that morning had no control over when they would be discovered. Priscilla could have found hers first if she hadn't been in a rush to open the coffee stand. Maybe the person assumed she would since she had to rise early. Then Wanda would have known it was about Debi from the get-go.

Wanda shook that idea from her brain. Another one filtered in. Maybe he or she had planned to kidnap Debi anyway. If she had been. No one knew for certain.

Even so, then why the time limit? Oh, good gracious. There had to be more clues out there.

"Wanda? Did you hang up?"

Betty Sue's voice pulled her back from that thought. "Oh, no. I'm still here. It is just that I figured out how to arrange the words to where they made sense. Frank got one, too. His message read *nine*. So, all together it read, *Debi better stop report before nine*."

"This morning?"

"I am not sure. Tom says *The Gazette* goes to print at nine every Thursday night."

Betty Sue let off a small gasp. "Tonight."

"Yep."

"Wanda. Then why would she disappear now. It's only five? You said we weren't fast enough."

Wanda locked her front door and walked to the double driveway that joined hers and Evelyn's properties just in time to notice Evelyn backing out her car from the garage. "I guess whoever is behind this felt we weren't getting the message?"

"That doesn't make sense, though."

"I know." Wanda sighed. "Look, Betty Sue. Stay at Better Burgers. Evelyn and I are on the way. We can talk then."

Betty Sue agreed, and they hung up.

After Wanda climbed into Evelyn's car, she let her know the latest news. Evelyn appeared as perplexed as Betty Sue had sounded. "Why kidnap her before nine then? Something doesn't add up. Maybe we still have the message wrong."

"Let's swing by Priscilla's and get hers. Maybe if we can eyeball all of them together, we can make heads or tails of this mess."

"Deal."

A rumble of thunder rolled over the buildings and a flash of lightening whitened the street for a split second. Storms moved through North Texas in minutes, but that didn't mean they didn't pack a wallop. A parking spot directly in front of the Grocery Mart stood vacant as they arrived.

"Thank you, Jesus." Evelyn winked as she pulled in.

Wanda whispered an *amen* and dashed inside to get the note. She returned a few minutes later with it in hand as quarter-sized raindrops splattered the sidewalk. The two drove west on Main toward Better Burgers in silence while the windshield wipers tapped out a rhythmic beat. The blades added a percussive *screech* against the dampening glass.

"Weatherman missed this one." Evelyn parked and then reached across Wanda for her foldable umbrella in the glove box. "Here, I'll share." She got out, whipped it open, and dashed around the back of the car to Wanda's passenger side.

"Thanks." Wanda ducked under as she exited the vehicle. Then the two skedaddled in unison to the awning over the entrance.

As they entered, the hum of human conversation, the clanking of dishes, and the aroma of French fries and sizzling onions blasted their senses. A milkshake machine whirred behind the counter and the old-fashioned cash register made a ding as the till slid open.

Wanda and Evelyn saw Betty Sue sitting at a table. She noticed them and waved. As soon as they had seated, she called Keith over.

"I told Keith about these mysterious notes."

Wanda dug into her purse and unfolded them onto the table. "Here they all are. Keith, do you recognize the handwriting at all?"

A usually athletic young man now appeared ten years older, at least. His shoulders bent forward, carrying the weight of his worry. He lowered himself into the chair he'd pulled over. Wanda watched his hands tremble as he moved the pieces of paper around the table.

"Um, no. It is almost as if it was printed, but not."

"I agree." Wanda tapped the one with Debi's name. "Can't decipher if it is written by a man or a woman, can you?"

"No. *Debi Better Stop Report Before Nine.*" The furrows on his forehead deepened. "I don't get it."

"Do you know of a story or a lead she's working on? Anything scandalous or incriminating?"

He scoffed and leaned back. "She writes articles on things that matter. Social issues. I guess that might ruffle a few feathers."

One could detect the pride in his eyes as he spoke. Wanda saw a deep affection there as well. Debi had landed a good one. Hardworking, honest, and totally enamored with her. Churchgoer, as well. For as long as she remembered, he and Todd had been in the same Sunday school classes growing up.

A deeper fervency to locate Debi bubbled up into her heart. She prayed the girl would be unscathed. "Have you notified the police?"

He ran a hand through his wheat-colored locks. "I did. It hasn't been very long, so she is not yet classified as a missing person though Reagan, the new dispatcher, did take down the information and told me to call back if she is still missing tomorrow. For all we know she could have had a flat on the highway or something."

"And not phoned you?" Betty Sue cocked an eyebrow. "Debi is more conscientious than that. She didn't get to be a state-wide known reporter without being responsible."

Evelyn interrupted. "Doesn't it have to be twenty-four or forty-eight hours before an adult is considered missing?"

Keith sighed. "I thought so but I called anyway. Seems that is a myth, though I think they might not go all out in investigating until it is certain that she is really missing. I mean she isn't a diabetic or mentally incompetent or whatever."

"Even so. This is not like her." Betty Sue sat more erect. "Wanda, call Todd. He should be on duty by now, right?"

"Not until six." Wanda glanced at her watch. "Which is in forty-five minutes. I'll invite him to come eat, and then, Keith you can talk with him, off the clock."

A grin cracked his worried expression. "Great."

Wanda chuckled "I know how to entice him. I have

these coupons your dad gave me when I got the civic award from the mayor."

"Right, for helping to solve those murders." His face suddenly turned the color of Betty Sue's vanilla shake, what was left of it. "Wait. Did this guy, or whoever, pick you three out to receive the notes on purpose? Please, tell me you don't think . . ."

She pressed her hand on his arm. "No, not in the least. This is a harmless prank. I am sure of it."

Betty Sue and Evelyn nodded in affirmation. But Wanda could tell from their eyes that they were not so sure.

Truth be known. Neither was she.

CHAPTER EIGHT

Todd never could turn down a free meal. Probably not many single guys could. He pulled in just as the storm passed overhead.

Shaking the droplets from his Stetson, he parked it on the hat stand and sauntered over to where Wanda and her friends sat. "Ladies."

"Pull up a chair. There's room." Wanda motioned for him to sit next to her. "I ordered you a double chili cheeseburger with onion rings and a Coke. Keith will bring it over in a minute."

A smile crossed his lips. "Okay, what's up now?" He glanced at each of them with narrowed eyes. "You three are up to something."

"Guilty." Wanda dug the notes out from her purse. "We each got one of these today. So did Hazel, Frank, and Priscilla. Do you know of anyone else who received them?"

"You mean in the mail?" Todd flipped through them without shifting his attention to his aunt's face.

"Nope. On our windshields." Betty Sue sniffed. Rainy weather always triggered her allergies.

"Between nine and ten this morning from what we can gather." Evelyn squirmed closer to the table.

"One of these words is *nine*."

"Yeah, we know. We don't really know what any of them mean, except there has been a new development."

"I know." Todd sat back as Keith brought his food. He raised his gaze to the new burger place owner. "Debi should be here, but she isn't."

Keith almost spilled the cola as he set it down. "How did you know?"

Todd smirked. "We do communicate at the station, but are you certain she isn't on assignment in Austin or Houston and forgot to tell you?"

"No. She said she'd meet me here at one." He pounded his finger into the laminated tabletop as his voice wobbled. "We were to go over some things for the wedding. She'd have told me if she had a change of plans."

Todd raised his hand. "Okay, man."

Wanda grabbed her nephew's sleeve. "Surely these notes add a sense of urgency to the situation."

He turned to face her. "Do you know who wrote them?"
"No."

"Well then, how can you determine these are meant to be sinister?"

Wanda opened her mouth to answer but Keith interrupted. "Because Debi is missing," he said with a quiver in his voice.

Todd gazed up at him. "Missing? You're absolutely sure?"

Keith must have recognized the sharpness in his answer. He stopped and took a deep breath. His voice quivered. "She said she'd be here at one. It's almost six. It's not like her. She thrives on punctuality. Says it's her middle name."

Todd stood and wrapped his arm around Keith's shoulders, which had drooped considerably. "Hey, man. I get it. It is definitely not characteristic of your fiancé. That's why we've already contacted the area hospitals and the Department of Public Safety to make sure no person matching her description has been in an accident."

"You . . .you have?" Keith's eyes held a pleading expression. "And . . .?"

"Nothing. But that doesn't mean she's missing. Not yet."

The young man's knees buckled into the chair Todd had occupied next to Wanda. "Where could she be?"

Todd leaned in. "I will keep an eye out and an ear to the ground tonight on my patrol, okay? In the meantime, if you hear from her, let me know."

"Thanks, man." Keith rubbed his forehead.

Wanda smiled. His hands smelled like French fries. She recalled when Todd worked there in high school and often came home wearing that aroma. Keith's dad had given him the job back then to help get his mind off his parents' divorce.

"No problem. Listen, bag mine to go, okay?" Todd slapped his back.

Keith leapt to attention. "Of course." He grabbed the tray and rushed away, back into restaurant manager mode.

Todd turned to Wanda. "You ladies enjoy your meal. Thanks for the freebie, Aunt Wanda."

He brushed his lips against her cheek, which made Wanda blush with joy. Todd was like a son to her. During the nasty divorce, his dad had left town with another woman to avoid scandal. Her sister left Todd in Wanda's care during his awkward teens so she could find a new life away from the small-town gossipers. Playing word games became the glue that bonded Wanda and Todd. It slowly mended their cracked hearts.

She recovered her composure by brushing invisible lint off his police uniform shirt. "Don't get any chili on your shirt. The grease will be a doozy to get out."

"Yes'm." He winked at her friends. "Oh, and if you discover at the neighborhood watch meeting tonight that anyone else has received notes like these, let me know."

She bobbed her head rapidly. "Promise."

Todd bore into her eyes a minute, then broke his gaze and turned to meet Keith headed that way with his sack and drink. He leaned into Keith's ear and whispered loudly. "Don't tell Aunt Wanda you usually give me free meals anyway."

Wanda's mouth dropped open. Of course, he would.

Todd was not only a police officer in Scrub Oak but one of Keith's close friends.

Keith winked, the color returning to his usually ruddy cheeks.

Todd laughed and grabbed his Stetson in his other hand before pushing open the door to enter the damp and cool evening.

Julie B Cosgrove

CHAPTER NINE

Wanda gathered the notes together, then she and Evelyn headed for the meeting. Betty Sue followed in her car. Evelyn and Betty Sue were not captains but, since they had received notes and were watch volunteers, Wanda invited them. They arrived at Holy Hill Church just as Pastor Bob opened the doors to the fellowship hall.

Several of the eight neighborhood watch captains had already pulled into the parking lot, and they joined in as they strolled up the steps to the double doors. The aroma of fresh coffee greeted them, along with a plate of peanut butter chocolate chip cookies, no doubt baked by Mary Lou Fitzgerald, the organist and now part-time secretary since she retired from teaching to have a baby. Since she only worked from nine to one, she'd obviously set the timer on the urn to begin brewing before their arrival.

"That dear lady is a gem." Jerry, one of the captains, winked as he grabbed a cookie.

"Yes, she is." Wanda took a cookie as well. "How she

does everything she does with a small toddler to care for while her husband is serving in Iraq is beyond me."

"Mmm hmm." He poured some coffee into a takeaway cup. "By the way, Melissa can't come tonight. One of the rabbits is delivering."

"Understandable." He and Melissa lived at the edge of town and if anyone found a hurt animal, they brought it to them to care for. Wanda grinned and went to greet the others who had arrived, including Frank who gave her a small wave before cupping his face in his elbow to cough.

After five minutes, she pounded the gavel to start the meeting. Pastor Bob lead them in prayer, then turned the meeting over to her.

Wanda let each captain give their bi-weekly report. A rattling in the Wardens' backyard had turned out to be a family of raccoons visiting their trash cans. Two teens were seen with spray paint cans in their hands but dropped them on the curb when confronted and hustled off. Their names were given to the principal. The branches to an elm on the corner of Main and 4th was blocking the stop sign's visibility and several residents have complained. The tree was in the city easement, not the property owner's front yard. Wanda promised to let the city council know.

She then addressed the room. "Ladies and gentlemen, today several Scrub Oak residents, including myself, received strange one-word notes on the windshields of their cars. Has anyone else received one or have heard of anyone in their neighborhood receiving one? Especially in the northeast quadrant."

Murmurs filtered through the fellowship hall and several heads shook in response.

"Okay." Wanda glanced at Tom Jacobs, who had arrived as *The Gazette's* reporter. He stared back at her in silence after viewing something on his phone. Could it be about Debi?

Something in his eyes told her he had information he didn't wish to share with the group. She made mental note to corner him after the meeting. She returned her attention to the room.

"Well, if you hear of any, please bring them to me. I am gathering them for the police, just in case." Movement on her right caught her eye as Tom slipped out the exit. What was that all about?

Fix-It Finn raised his hand. "What's this we hear about Debi Castro going missing?"

Wanda swallowed. She pondered how much to tell them at this point. "Todd spoke with her fiancé, Keith, a little while ago. He assured Keith that none of the hospitals or the highway patrol has reported anyone matching her description as being involved in an accident. So that is good news."

Everyone's shoulders seemed to relax a little. In a small town, concern ran deep, and news spread like water from a leaky hose across a concrete driveway.

"Had they had a fight or something?" Collin Rollins enquired as he raised his hand, per meeting protocol.

"Keith didn't indicate that they had." Wanda glanced around the room. "Anything else?"

Larry spoke up. His wife, Barbara, was the town librarian and secretary for the City Council. "Should we be thinking about the Halloween festival coming up next month? Do we need extra patrols for that night?"

Wanda widened her eyes. "You know, I had not thought about that, but it is a good question. What does everyone else think?"

A fifteen-minute discussion ended with an almost unanimous agreement that the captains should join the regularly scheduled watch persons that night in their quadrants and also give every child under the age of thirteen a postcard with Halloween safety tips along with a lollipop taped to each one. Betty Sue volunteered to help design the cards and Wanda told them she'd ask if Tom Jacobs would print them at no cost. Jerry said he and Melissa would get the lollipops at the wholesale store and tape them on.

Collin suggested they hand out the cards to every household a few days before Halloween to make sure the parents read the safety tips and discussed them with their kids. It would be a good reminder to the neighbors of who their captain was. Everyone unanimously agreed to have them passed out to all families with young children door-to door on the 29th of October.

With that the meeting adjourned.

Wanda stepped down from the podium platform. She searched the small crowd to see if Tom had returned. Maybe he'd stepped out to answer a phone call.

"What's wrong?" Evelyn stopped her.

"Did you see Tom Jacob's face when he left earlier? It was as if he knew something but wasn't going to speak up."

"You mean about Debi?"

"Possibly." Wanda leaned against one of the folding tables. "Some report has to be stopped from being printed tonight. But which one?'

Evelyn scoffed. "Well, obviously one Debi was working on. You need to go speak to Tom right now."

"True. I need to approach him about the printing anyway. Y'all want to tag along?"

Betty Sue shook her head. "I have to head into Fort Worth early in the morning for a doctor's appointment."

"I'll come." Evelyn grabbed her purse. "I drove anyway, remember?"

"Right. Let's clean up quickly and then head over to *The Gazette*."

When they got there, the lights were on, but no one answered their knocks. Wanda couldn't peer through the glass because the blinds were down.

"He has to be here. His car is over there." Evelyn pointed to a navy sedan parked on the Ash Ave side of the building.

The two women walked around for a closer look. That's when they noticed the employee entrance door wedged open with a box. A thin triangle of yellow light filtered out onto the street. The sound of a copier whirring stopped abruptly. Then a loud thump, thump, thump, and a clunk echoed out to their ears.

"What was that?" Evelyn shuffled to the door.

Wham.

It flew open and crashed against the brick building.

Evelyn gasped.

A shadowy figure in a black hoodie pushed her backwards to the ground and ran down the street.

Wanda would never forget the sound of her friend's skull cracking against the concrete.

Peanut Butter Chocolate Chip Cookies

Ingredients

- 2 cups sifted flour
- 1 cup brown sugar
- 1 cup sugar
- ½ teaspoon salt
- ½ teaspoon cream of tartar
- 1 teaspoon baking powder
- 1 cup butter, softened
- ¾ cup peanut butter (crunchy if you wish)
- 2 large eggs
- 1 teaspoon vanilla

- ¼ teaspoon almond extract
- 1 11.5-ounce bag of semi-sweet chocolate chips
- 1 cup finely chopped pecan pieces if desired

Instructions

Preheat oven to 375° F.

1. Mix dry ingredients together, then fold in the eggs, extracts, butter, and peanut butter until blended. Add in chocolate chips and pecans.
2. Refrigerate for an hour, then spoon dollops onto parchment paper laid over a cookie sheet.
3. Bake for 12-14 minutes per batch.
4. Cool each batch for 5 minutes then transfer to a baker's rack to cool further.

Makes 2-3 dozen, depending on the size of the cookies.

Julie B Cosgrove

CHAPTER TEN

Wanda rushed to Evelyn's side.

Her friend lay flat on the ground as a small groan eked through her half-parted lips.

Wanda dialed Todd's cell phone.

"Hurry. I think *The Gazette's* been vandalized and the perp just escaped after knocking Evelyn out. Call an ambulance, too."

Wanda wiped tears from her eyes as she felt for a pulse. Weak, but steady. Hers, however, thumped in her ears.

"Help is on the way, Ev. Hang tight."

Her friend's eyes stared straight ahead, cloudy.

Hurry, Todd. Wanda bent her head and prayed as she held her friend's hand. Tears rolled down her cheeks and splattered in drops onto concrete as the clock in the courthouse tower a few blocks away struck nine o'clock.

Sirens blared. She raised up to see a police cruiser barreling down the street along with the fire chief's, Adam Archer, SUV. He pulled to a stop and dashed out with his emergency kit. Todd followed.

Todd grabbed her shoulders and lifted her to stand. "You okay?"

She nodded and sniffed. "Evelyn."

"On it." He squeezed her arm, then bent to observe her lifeless friend sprawled over the stoop, face up on her back with her head slanted down into the alley. Her countenance appeared gray, and her eyes non-focused.

Wanda stepped back, her lip tucked in her teeth and her arms wrapped tightly around her torso.

Archer gazed up at Todd. "She's semiconscious. BP is dropping, though. Pulse weak. Let's get her to the Med Center."

"Right."

Archer wrapped Evelyn's neck in foam to stabilize it as Todd grabbed a flatbed transporter from the back of the chief's van and lowered the back seats.

They counted to three and lifted her onto the transport, then slid her inside the SUV. Todd came over to Wanda. "You think you can drive?"

"She did. I don't have her keys." Her voice quivered. She hated for Todd to see her so rattled.

Todd spun around and then noticed Evelyn's purse on the street next to the curb, a few of its contents spilled. He gathered them up and handed it to his aunt. "Here. Her keys are probably in there."

Wanda dug until she heard metal rattling. She nodded and pulled out Evelyn's keychain.

"Can you drive her car over there?"

She swallowed to gain more composure. "It's only two blocks, Todd. I can manage."

"Let's go, Todd." Archer waved for him to crawl in the back of the SUV.

"You go on. Need to stay here and secure the scene."

Archer gave him a thumbs up, closed the door, and climbed into the driver's seat. He peeled out, his tires spewing small pieces of road gravel. One stung Wanda's leg.

"You sure you are okay to follow? You really look pale."

She straightened her spine. "I'm fine. But at the hospital I'll only be in the way. Let me help you here."

"Huh-uh. I've already called it in. Chief Brooks is on the way. The vein on his forehead would pop if he saw you poking around."

They heard a screech of tires and turned to see the chief's cruiser jolt to a stop. He exited and walked briskly over to them. "Report."

Todd filled him in.

Brooks turned to Wanda. "Can you describe the guy? I assume it was a man."

"I believe so. Yes. Young, but not a teenager. Tall, thin, dressed all in back. Had on a hoodie so I didn't see his face. It all happened so very, very fast."

She suddenly felt the shakes ripple through her body.

Todd led her to a group of plastic crates stacked by the

trash cans near the back door. He upturned one and brushed it off with his sleeve. "Shock is settling in. Here. Sit. Take deep breaths."

Brooks entered the building, then stopped on the stoop. "Martin."

Todd raised up. "Sir?"

"I need you." His chief stepped gingerly inside. Todd followed but halted. "Wow."

Wanda stood, felt her knees hold her balance, and then took three steps to peer around Todd's side. She gasped.

The inside of *The Gazette's* printing area lay in shambles. Papers were strewn over the floor. The intruder must have emptied all the copies trays and half the filing cabinets onto it. The industrial style off-set printer with its four towers looked as if someone had sledgehammered it in several places. Like a broken Goliath on the Philistine plains, it lay dark and quiet.

Then, as Todd moved forward, careful not to disturb the littered floor, she saw it. Unmistakable. One arm of Tom's long sleeved, gray plaid shirt peeking through the debris. Her eyes followed the clump of papers to find his black shoes, toes against the floor.

They didn't move.

Brooks bent down on one knee over the heap, cleared a few papers with his gloved hands, and reached to place two fingers on Tom's neck.

"Is he?" Wanda couldn't bring herself to say the word.

Brooks glanced up. "Found a pulse. Call an

ambulance."

Todd did.

Then the chief's focus landed onto Wanda. He pointed at her as his cheeks flushed a bright red and a vein bulged on his balding brow "And get her out of here. Cordon off the room. This is a crime scene for goodness sakes."

"Yes, sir."

Todd's face reddened as he gazed at his aunt.

Message received. She backed out of the door onto the stoop again. The wobbliness returned to her knees. She braced herself on the jamb. Then realizing she'd left her fingerprints, she whispered "sorry", wiped her hands on her slacks, and stumbled the rest of the way to the alley.

Todd came and rested his hands on her shoulders. "Steady now." In a low, soft voice he continued as he gazed into her eyes. "Go to the hospital. Check on Evelyn, okay? Let us handle this. After we've made sure Tom has been transported and the scene locked down, I'll come by and get your official statement."

She squeaked out an okay. With all the control she could gather, she managed a small smile and a wink to reassure him she wasn't a wimpy wuss.

His eyes warmed. "That's my aunt." Then he went to his car to get the police tape.

Another siren's pulsating whine, in a different pitch, grew louder. The county ambulance pulled up and two EMTs jumped out.

Wanda shuffled to Evelyn's car and slumped against it.

Red and blue lights from all the emergency vehicles reflected on the damp pavement, pulsing at slightly different speeds. It made her head swirl.

Hot tears stung her eyes as she blinked. Two friends had been seriously injured. One citizen was missing, which left her fiancé heartbroken. Another tragedy had occurred in her town, and once again Wanda felt helpless to do anything about it.

Why here? Why Me?

She bowed her head and prayed . . . for Tom, for Evelyn, and for Debi Castro, wherever she was.

Suddenly, something inside her surged. A thought, no more than that, sounded in her brain. *Because you can.*

Resolve oozed through her sinew. A new strength coursed through her veins.

She straightened, grabbed her phone, and group texted the captains to be on the lookout for a tall, thin male, dressed all in black, with a hoodie, and last seen on foot fifteen minutes ago heading east on Ash.

Contact every neighborhood watch person ASAP. Comb the town, the fields, the lake resort area, and the railroad tracks. Cruise the highway. When spotted, dial 9-1-1, then text me.

Whoever was doing this wouldn't get away with it. Not in her community.

He'd picked the wrong Texas town to mess with.

CHAPTER ELEVEN

Wanda sat in the emergency waiting room. Minutes after she'd arrived the EMTs had pushed through with a still lifeless Tom on the gurney. At least his head wasn't covered with a sheet. That meant something.

She huffed a breath out of her cheeks and stood to stretch some of the tension from her muscles. A soft voice came up behind her and startled her.

"Looks like you could use this."

She swiveled to see a young woman in scrubs with her hair in a ponytail holding a takeaway cup. The aroma of freshly brewed coffee hit Wanda's senses. Her hand grasped the steaming cup and raised it to her nose. Ahh, nothing smelled so good as coffee. Unless it was that awful stuff . . ..

Wait a minute. Wanda spun around. Thoughts crammed into her head so fast that she couldn't even put them into words.

"Are you all right? Did it burn you?" The nursing student took the cup back.

"Uhh." Her mouth just hung open, unable to say anything. She dug in her pocket for her phone. "I have to make a call." She glanced up at the young woman. It was the best apology she could give as she punched in her nephew's phone number.

"I'm heading there right now, Aunt Wanda," Todd answered without even saying *hello.*

"Coffee." The words were beginning to fall into place in her head.

"I'm sure the nurse's station has some, or there's a vending machine."

"No." She needed to make him understand. "I remembered something. The young man in the hoodie that pushed Ev down. He smelled like coffee. And not just any coffee. Ugandan Supreme."

Todd's voice slipped into business tone. "That horrid syrup from this morning."

"Yes." Silence. "Todd?" She spotted the lights of his car as the call dropped.

He pulled alongside her, got out of the cruiser, and then joined her on the curb. "Are you sure about the smell?"

She glanced up at him. "Wouldn't you be?"

He pushed his Stetson back off his brow. "And only Priscilla carries it."

"As far as I know. She says it's selling like hot cakes. Hard to believe though." She wrinkled her nose.

"How did she get the boxes? By delivery truck or the post office?"

"I think she said they were delivered. Want me to call her?"

Todd glanced at his watch. "It's only 9:45. Yeah. Now."

Glad to have something to do, Wanda punched in another button on her phone. A groggy Priscilla answered at the other end. "Hello?"

Of course, she'd gone to bed early. The lady had to open at six in the morning. Wanda apologized for calling so late.

"It's okay." The reply came out in a yawn. "I hadn't gotten to sleep just yet."

"Priscilla, how do you get your Ugandan Supreme?"

"Huh?"

"Is it shipped to the grocers, or do you have to pick it up?"

"Why? Do you want to order some more?"

Wanda gulped back her instinctive response. "Um, no. Todd wants to know. He is looking into how and when someone put those notes on our cars." She glanced at Todd and grimaced.

He shrugged and mouthed back. "Not totally a lie."

Wanda rolled her eyes and put the call on speaker.

"Oh. Well, um, usually I order online, and it is delivered to the Grocery Mart, yes. But this shipment was different. I got a text early this morning saying they were short of drivers and if I needed it today, I could come pick it up at their warehouse in Cleburne. I sent one of the grocery stockers to get it and he delivered them later this morning."

"The Ugandan coffee is manufactured here in North Texas?"

"No, no, dear Wanda. I mean the shipping company's local distribution center."

Wanda cupped her hand over the phone and whispered in Todd's ear. "And it seems someone knew that."

"How do you figure that?"

She shooed his question off and returned to Priscilla. "Thank you, hon. I'll tell Todd. Sleep tight."

She pocketed her phone and then turned her attention to him. "Elementary, my dear Martin."

This time he rolled his eyes.

She ignored his gesture and continued in a fake British accent. Since she'd lived in North Texas all of her life, her attempt at the Queen's English sounded more like a cockney southern belle from Lubbock. "The person who left the notes knew that she'd have to get someone else to go get her delivery. Thus, her car would be there at nine."

He shifted his weight. "Or he happened upon her car at nine-ish and figured she'd be too busy inside to see him slide it under her wiper."

"Maybe. But then why did Tom's attacker smell like this latest blend from Africa?"

Todd scratched his chin. "That is a good question. Do you recall anything else?"

"I didn't really see his face, Todd. It was dark and he

had his head half-hidden under that hoodie as he zipped out the door. Wait." She closed her eyes and massaged her temples. "When he knocked Ev down, he stopped, just for a split second."

"And?"

"And turned around to watch her fall." Wanda reopened her eyes as her pulse quickened. "It's as if I can almost see the face but not quite."

Todd slapped her on the back. "Good girl. Would you mind coming to the station right now and walking through the computerized sketch program? A visual may help."

She climbed into his police cruiser, the excitement of once again being useful on a case building in her heart. In fact, she could get used to this. Was sixty-seven too old to go to police detective school, if there was such a thing?

As he drove, he called the chief to let him know the shock had worn off, and they were headed to the station to see if anybody in the FBI or State's DMV database would jog Wanda's memory.

"Do you think someone will?" She stared at the station sign just ahead.

"Worth a try. The Department of Motor Vehicles can match driver's licenses. The state legislature passed a law several years back that allowed the FBI to access the front with the picture ID that gives the name, date of birth, and address. That means we can access the FBI's database and view it as well. The law enforcement officers, I mean." Todd raised his chest. "And not everyone. I just got my clearance last week."

"Really?" Pride swelled her heart to double its size. "Convenient timing."

"Hmm. Well, God works in ways we don't always understand."

"Amen." Wanda grinned. Humility always had oozed from Todd's DNA. One of the reasons people warmed to him so quickly.

He parked and walked her toward the door, then gestured her to wait while he entered the building and punched in the passcode to turn off the alarm. A moment later the fluorescent lights flickered through the blinds. Todd stuck his head out of the doorway. "All clear. *Entre vu.*"

She gave him a small curtsy. "*Merci.*"

The room held an authoritative smell. Partly the odor of men, paper, floor cleaner, and stale coffee. Maybe fingerprint ink? No, that was digitally achieved now. But there whiffed through the area something she couldn't quite identify.

"This way." Todd motioned her into a small office, more like the size of a modest walk-in closet. Eight by eight feet at most. But it had a desk, office chair, and another chair angled to the side for guests . . . or suspects? A calendar courtesy of Hardware Haven on Main and 7th hung on one wall, and a poster to not text and drive on the other. A computer screen perched at an angle on the desk. A stack of folders and papers cluttered most of the surface.

Wanda spotted a crossword puzzle booklet on top along with a can of Coke and a paper plate with a half-eaten slice of pizza. "So, I finally get to see your office, huh?"

"Um, yeah. Got it a few weeks ago."

"Good for you. No doubt the reward for helping solve four murders, one that had been unsolved for more than a decade." She smiled, glad her stealthy efforts had helped seal his position on the Scrub Oak Police Department.

The back of his neck blushed when he removed his Stetson and hung it on the peg along with his police belt.

That was the unidentified aroma she had sniffed earlier — leather mixed with a blend of men's aftershave or hair products. How did Reagan, the only female in the place, stand it day in and day out? Maybe she should bring her a vanilla candle or a can of air freshener. It would be a nice welcoming gift for her since she was their newest recruit.

He motioned her to scoot the chair closer to the desk and angled the computer screen so she could view it better. After a half hour, the two of them came up with a rendering that satisfied Wanda. A slender face, dark eyes, and dark hair. Tan or light brown complexion, perhaps Hispanic.

"Okay. Let's see if we have any possible matches. Nothing firm, mind you. But it will be a start."

He punched in a code and uploaded the rendition into the FBI database. "It was pretty pricey, but the Feds gave us a huge discount as a thank you for our help in ending Butch McClain's crime spree."

McClain had been one of the instigators in the

Ferguson Mansion case. Wanda felt her chest swell again. She had insisted the well-known criminal had to be involved and that hunch had proved to be right.

It didn't take long for five profiles to pop up on the screen. Two were in Michigan, one in Nevada, and one in New Jersey. Todd clicked some more keys. "Oops, forgot to set some parameters."

Wanda tapped the screen. "That's okay. It narrows it down to this guy from Texas and I think he looks more like the young man I saw than the others."

"Juan Estrada from Elgin, TX. That's a good two hours plus drive from here."

"Well, maybe he moved, or found a job up here. Or, if he is a delivery driver, he could have the route from Austin to the Metroplex. Elgin isn't that far from the airport down there."

Todd stroked his chin. Wanda knew the wheels in his head were turning. Todd had been in Austin for the police academy and knew the area as well as the usual riff raff.

"Does he look familiar, Todd?"

"Huh? Um, not really." He leaned closer to the monitor. "Let's check his social media footprints."

Chapter Twelve

As Todd searched and scrolled, Wanda watched him surf for data about the guy, his life, and his friends. It proved a bit unnerving to discover how easy it was to find information about anyone. Up until now, Wanda thought it fun to reconnect with people from her past. Plus, she had made some internet friends from all over the country who also liked word games. She played and chatted with several online from time to time. Could anyone read that?

Oh, my heavens. Wanda decided she had been too present and transparent in her personal postings.

"Well, you are correct." Todd sat back, and his office chair creaked in response. The sound echoed through the empty station. "He has friends in the metroplex. An aunt in Burleson. And get this." Todd pointed to the screen. "He drives for a major delivery company."

"May I take a picture with my phone and show it to Evelyn when she is more awake?"

"Sure. Also, I want to confiscate her clothing to see if

by some chance he left a fingerprint on the fabric."

"You can do that?"

"I can't. Forensic teams can. And two people have been assaulted, not to mention property destroyed, so the request is warranted. Of course, they usually handle their caseloads first so it may take a while. But it's worth the shot."

Wanda grinned at the idea of Evelyn in one of those hospital gowns, then her smile quickly reversed as the sides of her mouth drooped.

"What is it?" Todd gazed at her, the illumination from the computer screen outlining his chiseled cheekbone.

She turned to him, rubbing her hands in her lap. "This is way too easy. It's never this easy, is it?"

Todd crossed a knee over his leg as he stretched back in his chair. "Rarely."

"Yeah, that's what I thought."

Juan Estrada had no criminal record other than two speeding tickets as a teenager, six years prior. Not enough for him to disqualify for a commercial license. So why would he trash a county newspaper office and knock over a scrawny old lady? And why smell of foreign roast?

Wanda frowned. "I could be wrong, you know."

"About what?"

"His face. It happened so quick and in the dark. Maybe I've recall his face incorrectly."

Todd punched his fingers over the keyboard and swiveled the monitor toward her. Enlarged on the screen stood a photo of Juan with two friends. He wore a dark hoodie.

"Doesn't mean a thing. Thousands of kids wear those."

"True."

Wanda's phone chimed. She read the text. Ray O'Malley reported that a person matching the description had been seen running down the alley to Cottonwood Lane and jumping into a small white four-door sedan.

She showed it to Todd.

"Ask if he was a passenger or driving."

Wanda texted back Todd's question. The answer pinged. *Driver.*

"That means he was alone, right?"

"Yep." Todd rose from the desk and stretched. "White four-door sedans are the most common car on the road. Ask if he got a glimpse of license plate."

She did and the answer came back. *Not really. Too dark.*

"It was worth a shot."

She thumbed back a reply. *Todd says Okay. Thanks.*

"At any rate, I need to inform the chief. I'll see if there is word about Tom and Evelyn, too." He booted up his phone.

Evelyn. Wanda mentally slapped herself. How could she have forgotten one of her close friends lay in the hospital with a jostled noggin?

After he hung up with the chief, Wanda spoke.

"I better get back over there, Todd. I have her car. Well, I mean I have the keys."

"Right. I'll take you back. I need to go patrol the town. The chief wants to crisscross the area in our search now that we have some info."

"Gonna be a long night, then?"

"It's what we do, Aunt Wanda. But I'll be back to the hospital in an hour or so and come find you. If Tom comes to, we'll have to interview him. He is still in surgery."

"We?" Her mood lifted.

He flicked off the office light and closed the door. "The chief and I."

She ducked her chin. "Oh. Of course."

Todd's muffled chuckle hit her ears. She felt silly. Why would she assume she'd be in on that?

Her friends were right. Sometimes she did stick her nose where it didn't belong. Still, she planned to query Evelyn. Maybe she'd gotten a better glimpse of her assailant than Wanda had.

CHAPTER THIRTEEN

Evelyn was sitting up in a gurney, an icepack to her skull. Her eyes still seemed a bit cloudy and her skin too pale, even for her. Wanda gave her a small wave.

"Feel like company?"

Evelyn nodded then grimaced.

Wanda pulled up a chair and grabbed one of her friend's hands, the one without the pulse oximeter clamped to the forefinger. That's when she noticed one eye swelling and turning purplish. "What happened to your eye?"

"I think an elbow hit it, or perhaps the doorknob as I went down? I am not sure. It hurts worse than the back of my head though." Evelyn's voice sounded gravelly.

"I'm sorry."

"I had to have stitches." She pointed to the back of her head. "Seven."

"Ouch."

"The police took my clothes." Her tone became grouchier.

"I know. They needed them for evidence."

"Where have you been?"

Wanda opened her mouth then thought better. She didn't want Evelyn to think she mattered to her less that Debi did. "Can you have water?" She pointed to a Styrofoam and plastic pitcher on the bedstand.

Evelyn blinked. "Yeah. Sips. Now that they have run all their tests. My throat is dry as my lawn in August during a water ban."

Wanda poured a bit of water into a cup, unwrapped the plastic bend-straw, and handed both to her. "Todd had me come to the police station to see if my description of the guy who knocked you down matched anyone in the criminal database. And, no it didn't. But we did find a DMV photo that may be him."

She took a swallow and cleared her throat. "Anyone we know?"

"Unfortunately, no. But do you feel up to looking at his photo?" Wanda pulled out her phone.

Evelyn removed the ice bag. "Guess so. But I really didn't get a good look at him. I mean, I think it was a guy."

"Me, too." She held up her phone.

Evelyn squinted then groaned. "Oh, my head. It feels as if I ate a gallon of ice cream in ten seconds, except it is also pounding."

Just then the curtain swished back. A nurse entered. "Ma'am, Mrs. Joseph really is not up to visitors yet."

Wanda gathered her things. "Oh, okay. Should I head

for the waiting room and stay there until she is discharged? I have the keys to her car and can take her home."

The nurse shook her head. "Not yet. We are keeping her here overnight for observation."

Evelyn groaned louder.

Wanda patted her hand. "I'll take your car back and check on Tweety. Make sure he has water, seeds, and then cover his cage. Don't worry."

She replied in a weak *okay*.

"I'll be back in the morning. You rest."

"Bring me clothes. Sweats will do. The weatherman said the rain brought in a cold front. First of the season."

Wanda glanced at the TV hanging on the wall. A talk show host gave his monologue. 10:30. No wonder she felt exhausted.

As Wanda left, she turned back to wave. She saw residual fear and loneliness in her friend's eyes. Evelyn liked consistency and control. Being laid up in a hospital bed in a one-size-fits-nobody gown did not conform to her lifestyle pattern. But again, whose did it fit?

Maybe Betty Sue who always looked for the positive angle and exhibited a sense of excitement over new happenings, kind of like Tigger in the Winne the Pooh stories. But not meticulous, introverted Ev. She resembled Eeyore.

Wanda sighed as she noticed her reflection in the shiny floors. She did sort of look like Pooh. Too much honey. And chocolate shakes, and French fries, and donuts, cookies . . .

but enough of that. More important things required her attention right now.

As she walked out of the emergency clinic, she lifted her friend in prayer. *Lord, hold her hand tonight. And while you're at it, protect Todd and Chief Brooks on patrol. Oh, and give the doctors and nurses the skills to help Tom heal.*

She saw his wife, Misty, curled into one of the plastic chairs in the waiting room with her chin in her hand and her eyes blankly staring into space. Wanda went to sit with her for a while. It was the least she could do.

Tweety could wait.

Chapter Fourteen

By seven the next morning, Wanda had already received eight calls. People wanted to know why *The Gazette* wasn't on their stoop or in the grocery store. The captains wanted to know if the suspect had been apprehended. Frank wanted to know why she had gotten home so late.

Wanda maintained patience and answered their questions as quickly and vaguely as possible while her own questions filtered through her head. She wanted to know if Tom survived the surgery and if Evelyn's psyche survived being couped up in the emergency clinic overnight. After dumping kibble in Sophie's bowl, she threw on some clothes.

At Ev's, she found a decent pair of sweats and checked on Tweety. Fifteen minutes later she drove to the Medical Center. As the double doors whirred open, she saw a ragged-looking Todd exiting. "Todd, how's it going?"

He raised his head and nodded it slightly in greeting.

Then he hooked his arm through her elbow and led her to one of the entry benches.

After they had been seated, he narrowed his gaze. "Tom is in ICU, but his vitals are stable. Lost his spleen, broke a few ribs, has a punctured lung, and has lost a lot of blood. A pretty serious concussion, too. They've put him in a medical coma until the brain swelling goes down. It'll be a few days before we can speak with him."

"And Ev?"

"Driving the nurses batty." He winked as he twirled his Stetson in his hands.

"I better go check on her." Wanda kissed his cheek and rose.

He blushed and glanced around as he rubbed her lipstick imprint off. "Sheesh, Aunt Wanda. Not in public. I'm not ten anymore."

She laughed. "When you were ten, you'd wouldn't let me within five feet of you for fear I'd smooch you, hug you, or wipe the grime off your face."

"I was smarter back then." He mumbled his response but not quietly enough for her not to hear.

She play-slapped his arm and headed to rescue Evelyn. Then she swiveled back as Todd got up to leave. "Hey, Todd. Wait."

He stopped, and his eyebrows pushed together.

She came toward him. "Any word of Debi?"

He glanced down at his boots and shuffled one of them across the shiny floor. "She's kinda low priority right now."

He raised his gaze and focused on her face. "Don't tell Keith that."

"Of course not. But what if the same guy who trashed *The Gazette* and assaulted Tom is responsible for her disappearance?"

"As far as I know no one has called for a ransom or anything like that. I haven't spoken to Keith. Have you?"

"Well, no."

"Maybe she showed up after all."

Wanda huffed. "Then why the notes?"

"No one produced any more at the meeting last night?"

"No. It seems just a few of us were targeted."

"You, Evelyn, Betty Sue, Frank, Hazel, and Priscilla."

"Right."

"I don't get it. Why y'all? It's not as if Debi was a close friend or relative to any of you."

"I know. That's what is so weird."

"Which reminds me. Exactly what were you and Evelyn doing at *The Gazette*?"

"Trying to track down Tom. He had been at the meeting, and I wanted to speak with him about Debi and see if he knew what she'd been working on. But he dashed out before I had a chance to corner him."

Todd harrumphed. "So, you followed him?"

"I had good reason, Todd. I knew he had to put the paper to bed. He told me that he wanted to get a blurb in about the neighborhood watch meeting to continue to drum up interest."

"And he was in a hurry to do so?"

"Exactly." Wanda focused on his face. "The paper always goes to print at nine on Thursday nights." She emphasized the word "nine" and saw Todd's expression change as he registered the meaning.

"The notes had said the report had to be stopped by nine."

She cocked one eyebrow. "And someone made sure it did, with or without Debi."

He rubbed a hand over his scalp and set his hat in place. "Well, in two more days, if she doesn't turn up, we can put out a clear alert."

"What's that?"

"It's like an Amber Alert for missing kids or Silver Alert for missing elderly. It'll be on the messaging billboards on all the highways as well as wired to the newspapers and TV and radio stations. Also texted to people statewide who sign up to get the alerts on their devices."

"Wow. That should help." Modern technology. Amazing. Her hope that Debi would be found raised a notch.

"In the meantime, take care of Evelyn. Let us talk with Tom when we are allowed to do so. He will most likely know what assignments she had going on. Maybe she will have some notes or something, though I bet it's all on her tablet or phone, which she probably has with her."

"Keep me posted?"

He waggled his finger. "Only if you promise not to go out on a limb and start snooping yourself."

She slapped her hand to her heart. "Moi?"

Todd gestured the "I am watching you" signal as he pointed to his eyes then hers. Then he left the building.

Wanda observed him walk to his cruiser. His demeanor oozed authority and his stride purposeful as he greeted some people coming in with a tip of his finger to the rim of his hat. How he'd grown into a fine young man.

Thanks to her previous sleuthing, along with the that of her friends, she had helped secure his reputation in the community as a competent law enforcement officer instead of the former lanky, introverted teen from a troubled family.

Now, she had the opportunity to do so again. Except he could never know it. She didn't want to anger him or alienate their close friendship by usurping his investigation. Afterall, he was her only local kin. Her own kids had long since flown the coop and settled into lives of their own. She was lucky to get together with them at Christmas and Skype with them now and then.

No, she had to keep on Todd's good side and still figure out a way to help him out by dropping hints in future conversations. Keep her foot in the door to make sure it stayed open.

Besides, she hadn't exactly promised she wouldn't snoop, had she?

Julie B Cosgrove

Evelyn's face had regained most of its color, though her eye had taken on many in the rainbow. A fresh gauze square and tape had been placed over the stitches in the back of her head. Her sour attitude meant she felt good enough to be discharged and anxiously waited for it to happen. Trouble was, that hospitals never ran on the patient's time.

"The doc came by hours ago. When will they let me out of here?" Her voice resembled a kid's whining about staying in detention.

"Patience. Certain things have to happen, like watching dominos tumble in those mazes. One has to collapse before the next one can."

"Ugh." She pouted with her arms crossed. "I cannot wait to have a long, hot shower. And get this antiseptic odor out of my nostrils."

"How's your head?"

She rubbed it. "Okay. Mild ache, but no dizziness. I believe I'm cognitive. I mean, I am conversing, right?"

Wanda laughed. "Yes, Ev. You seem your normal self. Just grouchier."

They heard the slight squeak of rubber soles and then the swoosh of the division curtains. "Mrs. Joseph? Here are your discharge orders. Let me go over with them to make sure you understand them, okay?"

Evelyn mumbled something undiscernible but listened with only a few sighs as the nurse went over the seven pages, all requiring her initials or signature.

"Now can I get dressed and leave?"

The nurse flashed her a sugary smile. "As soon as I make copies and order the wheelchair."

After she'd pulled the curtains, Evelyn groused. "In other words, we wait some more."

Wanda decided her friend needed a boost. "How about I find the cafeteria and bring you some fresh coffee and a warmed doughnut or muffin."

Her friend's eyes shined with new hope. "Wonderful. I couldn't swallow the gruel they brought earlier." She stuck out her tongue and shuddered.

Yep, the woman definitely needed sugar and carbs.

On her way to the cafeteria, Wanda took a detour into the waiting room. A disheveled Misty Jacobs sat curled into one of the armchairs, her head resting on her knees. She wore the same clothes as last night. Glazed-over eyes raised as Wanda approached.

"Hi, Misty. Is there anything I can do?"

She wiped a strand of hair from her cheek. "Pray?"

"Oh, believe me. Several of us have been. How is Tom?"

"Stable, thank the Lord. You and Evelyn Joseph found him, right? Thank goodness you did. He often stays until the wee hours getting the paper out so I wouldn't have suspected a thing until I noticed him not home the next morning. If he had laid there for hours, I . . ." Her eyes welled with fresh tears.

Her daughter, Vicki, handed her a tissue. Misty dabbed her eyes, long since void of make-up. "Anyway, thank you. How did you happen to be there?"

"I thought he might have some questions about the neighborhood watch meeting, and I knew he wanted to write a last-minute article about it."

She swallowed some water from a cone-shaped throw-away cup. "How is Evelyn? I hear whoever assaulted him injured her as well?"

"Fine. About to be released. I am on the way to the cafeteria to get her some fresh coffee. Can I get y'all anything?"

"No, thanks. We ate breakfast a while ago. Sweet of you to offer."

Wanda swatted her compliment away. "Do the police know anything?"

"No, not really. Tom is not lucid enough to give any testimony or whatever you call it."

"Who's running the Thrift Shop?"

Her daughter spoke up. "Dad has good part-time

employees who are putting in some extra time."

"That is serendipitous." Wanda smiled sweetly. "What about your fiancé? Is he on the way?"

"Dunno. Mason's awfully busy with his studies." She shrugged and picked a frayed thread from her jeans. Why kids paid mega bucks for ripped-in-the-knees clothes Wanda never did understand. But then, back in her day the current fashion seemed bizarre to her parents. Tie-dyes, peasant blouses, and love beads. Had she really worn those things?

"Listen. I don't know when the police will allow anyone into *The Gazette*, but I wanted you to know, I and several other ladies have time on our hands. We wouldn't mind sorting and filing papers back into the cabinets and cleaning up the place."

Misty uncurled her legs and sat up straight. "Seriously? Oh my, that would be so nice of you. I'd bring you lunch and snacks. Are you sure?"

"Absolutely. Just let me know when. You have my phone number? It's in the church directory."

She indicated that she did.

Wanda walked to the cafeteria with a new spring in her step. Kill two birds with one stone. Help a friend and also look for clues. Not bad. Pleased with herself, she decided to get two doughnuts, one for Ev and one for herself.

CHAPTER SIXTEEN

An hour later, Evelyn was wheeled out to her car before she shed blood and was arrested, which may have been a possibility if the delay had dragged on much longer. As Wanda drove her home, Evelyn gazed out the side window like a pampered dog who hadn't ridden in the car for months. Everything caught her attention anew as if she's been shut away for twelve years, not twelve hours.

After she got Evelyn settled, Wanda decided to head for Better Burgers. She wanted to talk with Keith about going with him to Debi's apartment. He'd probably prefer to have a woman go through her personal stuff.

Perhaps the girl had written down her contacts and appointments. Maybe they could glean something from her laptop if it were still there. If not, Betty Sue knew some techie kids at the high school who might know how to pull info from the damaged computers at *The Gazette*. One way or another, they had to find out what article seemed so damaging and to whom.

If they could get inside . . .

"I don't know." He rubbed his hands together, the whiff of French fries again reaching Wanda's nose. "I do have a key. Perhaps I should. I mean, under the circumstances, I don't think she'd mind, right?"

"Of course not. She gave you that key so you could have access. She trusts you."

"Okay. And I appreciate you going with me. Somehow having, well, pardon me for saying so, but an older woman with me seems more proper."

"Exactly why I volunteered. And no offense taken." Wanda pressed her lips into her sweetest little old lady smile.

"Gosh, I appreciate it. Things usually slow down about two. Can we go then?"

Wanda patted his arm for assurance the way Betty Sue did so often to her. "I'll be back then."

Worry melted from his face like a wax figure in a fire. It reassured Wanda that her intentions were true. Afterall, Debi had now been missing for 24 hours, her boss lay in ICU, and her workplace had been trashed.

Plus, someone had taken the time to stuff those words under their windshield wipers. And pick the receivers out, which meant they knew where to find them. If not someone local, they had to have access to a directory of some sort. Maybe subscription records? The newspaper was freely delivered to every resident but several people in the area supported it financially. She did, and so did Betty Sue.

Priscilla regularly had an ad in it. But Frank, Ev, and Hazel? She needed to ask them.

Something connected them all to the reason they had been chosen to receive the messages. But what? Those mysterious notes held the answer. If only she knew how to glean it.

It took Wanda and Keith only a few minutes to drive to the Lake View apartment complex. Keith kept fiddling with his key ring and caressing the one that unlocked Debi's apartment. Wanda figured he must really cherish her. Their marriage would be one that would last if they found Debi safe and sound. She sent up a silent prayer.

"Have you spoke to any of her family?"

His Adam's apple plunged as he swallowed. "No, not yet. I didn't want to worry them. I guess maybe I should now, though. Right? I mean after what happened last night, well, I don't mind telling you I'm freaked out by this."

He blinked back tears pooling in his lower eyelids, half-mooned by dark circles. The guy obviously hadn't slept. Wanda's heart melted. Poor thing. "Back in the day, my fiancé was missing in action during the end stages of Viet Nam, six weeks before his scheduled discharge date. Those five days were the worst in my life."

"Did he come home?"

"Yes, and we married. Had thirty-seven glorious years together." She smiled at him. "So will you two. At least."

He gulped and wiped his eyes. "I hope so." He pointed to the left. "She is in 648, that way. Park by the big oak tree."

They climbed the stairs that led to her second-story unit. Wanda glanced away as Keith's shaky hand fumbled with the lock. At last, he opened the door.

"Debi? Hon?" He peeked his head in. No answer.

Opening the door for Wanda, he motioned her inside. A slight scent of cinnamon and vanilla floated in the air from a dispenser plugged into the wall near the serving bar. The place appeared neat as a pin, but horridly still and silent.

"She's a good housekeeper, isn't she?"

Keith let out a small sigh. "Yeah. She likes everything neat and orderly. I have never seen it a mess."

Wanda wandered into the kitchen. The coffee pot had been rinsed. No dirty dishes lay in the sink. Counters wiped and gleaming. A scent of lemon detergent whiffed up when she flipped the lever and opened the door to the dishwasher to view sparkling glasses and plates. Debi must have run it before exiting the apartment. "Nothing seems array. She obviously didn't leave in a hurry."

"You mean she wasn't kidnapped from here, don't you?" Keith stood in the center of her small, square living room, his hand rubbing the back of his neck.

"Doesn't seem that way. No pet?"

"Um, no. Her cat died a few months ago. We were waiting until . . ." He stopped. His eyes scanned the room as if hoping to see something, anything that would be a clue to her whereabouts. His voice cracked. "Where could she be?"

"You look for a clue in here. See if there is a notepad, a scrap of paper, a calendar. I'll go check out her bedroom."

His jaw hardened, as if he now had a purpose. "Right."

Julie B Cosgrove

CHAPTER SEVENTEEN

Wanda entered Debi's tidy bedroom. The bed had been made, no wrinkles. Five throw pillows and two stuffed animals, obviously well-loved, were perched in a pleasing pattern. A student desk—placed to catch the sunlight from the window—held a pen holder, a stack of bills and envelopes, and a picture of Keith and her at the lakeshore. No desktop monitor or computer. Nowadays the younger set used tablets and phones, Wanda figured. She thumbed through the bills. Nothing out of the ordinary. Utility, cable, insurance.

Wanda reset the pile in the order she'd found it. Her eyes traveled the room and landed at the dresser. She walked over and pulled the top drawer open. Underwear. She pushed to close it again when something caught her eye.

She reached under a stack of folded undies and pulled out a flowery covered, bound notepad. Fanning the pages, Debi's upright, legible handwriting appeared on at least half. She turned to the last one and read the entry.

I am meeting with M tomorrow morning at sunrise at the designated spot. I hope we can see eye to eye. M has a lot at stake in this, too.

"Keith." Wanda rushed into the living room to find him sitting on the sofa staring at a piece of paper. His eyes reddened. He opened his mouth, but no words emerged. Instead, he held it up as if it contained something unthinkable.

Wanda took it and read. "Will meet you tomorrow morning at sunrise in the usual place. I hope your fiancé doesn't figure out we are meeting."

"What does it mean?" He squeaked out the question.

"I am sure it is nothing like you think. I'm betting it is work related. Look, I found this." She handed the opened notepad to him and stood there as he read the entry.

Keith set it on the coffee table as if it were made of the finest, most delicate crystal. He flopped back against the cushions and stared at the ceiling fan lowly whirring above him.

Wanda didn't know what to do. Stand there. Call Todd. Wrap the poor lad in her arms.

Without making eye contact he spoke in almost a whisper. "Who is M?"

"If you don't know . . . I mean you know all of her friends."

"This isn't a friend, is it?" He glanced at Wanda then back to the ceiling. Then he closed his eyes, buried them in his hands and groaned like a wounded animal.

"Keith?"

"I should have come here last night. Before nine. Told Tom. Called the police." He spoke so rapidly Wanda barely could keep up. She rounded the coffee table and sat next to him.

"Wondering about the woulda-shouldas won't help Debi now. Besides, from what these notes say she left yesterday morning, early. That means if something happened, and I am not saying it did, it occurred long before you were to meet at one."

"Yeah. I guess so. I feel like I have wasted precious time, though." Keith silently leaned forward with his hands now folded between his knees. As he did, a piece of paper appeared under the crushed cushion of the sofa where he sat.

Wanda pulled it slowly out. She unfolded it to reveal the numbers one through twenty, written one per line on the same type of notebook paper as the windshield notes had been written upon. Next to each number was capital letter. *A, B, B, C, A, D, B, C, D, A, E* and so on. On the side in Debi's handwriting was written *Proof? How to prove it? Ask M.*

"Those look like answers to multiple-choice questions on a test." Keith tried to snatch it from Wanda's hand, but she pulled it away. "No, it may contain fingerprints. Now it has mine along the edge. Let's not muddle things."

"Okay?" He scrunched his forehead.

"Our DMV records now have our fingerprints. I know

Todd has access to them. He showed me."

"So?"

She could tell Keith still didn't get it. Not that he was dense, the guy had smarts. He must just be distraught at the moment. She spoke slowly and clearly. "If the police can glean Debi's from her notepad, then maybe if there is another set . . ."

Hope sparkled in Keith's weary eyes as he interrupted her. "Aha. We will know who gave her this note."

"Exactly. Go see if you can find a big zip-bag."

He jumped from the couch as if he'd sat on a wasp and rushed into the kitchen. After shuffling through a few drawers, he waved from the serving bar that separated it from the open concept living/dining room. "Got some."

"Bring the box here."

He returned to the couch and pulled a bag out, then held it open as Wanda slipped the evidence inside, careful not to get more prints on it. Then she motioned for him to open another bag for the notebook and a third for the handwritten note he'd found.

Wanda winked. "Now we call Todd."

She decided not to tell Keith that the note about meeting Debi appeared to be in the same handwriting as on the cryptic windshield messages. Todd would pick up on that soon enough.

CHAPTER EIGHTEEN

Wanda answered the knock at the door, curious as to her nephew's reaction to her being there in Debi's apartment. He'd been nice enough on the phone, but she could never fully tell from his voice.

His smile wasn't large, but at least his eyebrows didn't meet in the center of his forehead.

"Hey, Keith." He acknowledged him with a sight head bob.

After inviting him inside, Wanda quickly briefed him on why she wanted him to come over. "Hmm, it sounds like a couple of good leads to me. You were right to call me."

Wanda's heartbeat slowed. "That's what Keith and I thought."

Already dressed in uniform, Todd took out a small black notepad from his utility belt. "Where is the note and the paper tablet you found?"

Wanda pointed to the coffee table where she had encased both in separate clear baggies. "We didn't touch them any more than necessary. And here is the notebook paper we found as well."

"Good job." He shot her a half grin.

She smiled back wondering why the mood shift. He appeared to be taking this all a lot more seriously. What did he know that he had not shared with her? Something important? Had Tom talked?

Irritation grew inside her mind. Why had Todd not phoned her, then? He'd promised to keep her posted. But then again, she had sort of promised she wouldn't sleuth. Maybe he played it cool now but would ream her out once they were in private for sticking her nose where it didn't belong.

Unless he had finally come to realize she only had his best interests at heart and was good at gathering information. One could only hope. She decided to smooth his feathers, just in case.

"Keith felt more comfortable asking a woman to look through Debi's, well, things. He thought we might find something that would let us know where she'd gone."

Todd wrote it down and glanced at his aunt. "Makes sense."

Keith, bless his heart, kept his lips pressed in a line.

Todd swiveled toward him, seated on the couch. "And you have no clue as to who this M-person might be?"

"Not really, Todd. I mean one of her roommates in college was named Margo. Then there is Morgan, another friend, who was a substitute teacher at the high school for

Mary Lou Fitzgerald."

Todd nodded. Mary Lou had gone through school with both Todd and Keith.

Keith continued. "But Morgan got a position in Abilene this year. She moved in July."

Todd scribbled some more in his pad. "That rules her out, I guess. Mary Lou starts with an *M*. Debi organized the meals for her after her baby came, right?"

Keith snapped his fingers. "Yeah. She did."

Wanda decided to address the proverbial gorilla in the room. "M could stand for a guy's name just as well."

"True." Keith's tone flattened. "We all knew Mike Gonzales in high school. Debi and I ran into him a few months ago in Fort Worth at Billy Bob's. He is an EMT tech now, going for his RN at UT Arlington."

Todd smiled. "Good for him. Anyone else?"

Wanda scrunched her shoulders. "Maybe Tom would know? I mean, if she was working on a story, perhaps she interviewed this M-person."

Todd side-glanced at her. "He is still not conscious enough for visitors. So, please don't try to visit him, okay? By the way, I know you volunteered yourself, Betty Sue, and Evelyn to go help clean up the mess at *The Gazette* and refile papers."

Here we go. Wanda lifted her chin. "We have the time. Just trying to be a good Christian neighbor."

"Uh, huh." His stare chilled her.

He turned his attention back to Keith. "May I have the

key to this apartment? I want to call in a forensic team from the county to go over it, just in case."

Keith's face became as white as a clown's makeup. "You think something happened here?"

Todd laid a grip on the man's shoulder. "Not necessarily. But they're better trained to discover clues than you two are. Of course, since you two have been rummaging through things, it may now be more difficult."

Wanda felt like shrinking into the wall socket, but she stood her ground.

Keith shot a glance at Wanda and then bobbed his head. "S-sure. Here." He twisted the key from his keyring. "Mrs. Warner, can you drive me back now? I need to prepare for the dinner crowd and place some produce orders to be delivered for tomorrow."

"Of course." She then addressed her nephew. "Thanks for coming over, Todd."

He peered into her eyes. "Thanks for telling me about this instead of going off half-cocked on a hunch."

She jutted her chin as she snatched her purse from the serving bar. "You're welcome. Let's go, Keith."

As they descended the stairs, Keith spoke up. "Is everything okay? I mean, did we do wrong by coming here?"

"Nah. Todd just worries that I will put myself or my friends in danger. He is being a bit overprotective. Truth is, I just seem to have a knack for running into clues."

"Oh."

She clicked her key fob to open the car door. "I keep telling him that I am a good resource, especially as head of the neighborhood watch in Scrub Oak. Reporting unusual things is my duty."

Keith didn't reply but climbed in the passenger seat. He remained quiet all the way back to Better Burgers. When she pulled in, all he said was, "Thanks, Mrs. W."

Wanda watched him slink into the restaurant like the statue of Atlas in Roman mythology who had the weight of the world strapped onto his back. Had she done the right thing by persuading him to go to Debi's place?

Surely so. But who was this M-person? Why did he want to meet Debi at dawn and not want Keith to know? And where was this *usual place*? It didn't sound very innocent. No wonder the guy worried over that note.

Wanda became convinced more than ever the answer lay at *The Gazette*. Even if it rattled Todd, she had to get in there and see what she could find. The police obviously were not inclined to do it at this point. Unless of course, the evidence she and Keith had found made a difference.

Time was of the essence. She rushed home to make her special deviled eggs to take to Tom's wife along with some peanut butter chocolate chip cookies.

Julie B Cosgrove

CHAPTER NINETEEN

Tom's wife didn't answer the door and her driveway was void of cars. Perhaps she still held vigil at the hospital. Wanda drove to the grocery and purchased some plastic containers. She divided the eggs and a few cookies into one then the rest of the eggs in another and the remaining dozen cookies in a third one. With a plan established, she waltzed into the medical center and punched the up button on the elevator.

"Oh." When the door opened, Todd stood there, his arms crossed. He held the door open for her. "Aunt Wanda."

She stammered. "I, um, saw Misty had not returned home, so I brought her some sustenance."

Todd glanced into the bag. "That's a lot of food."

"Well, you know how these recipes are. Serves eight. So, I thought the nurses' station might like some, too."

He pressed the button to the third floor. "She is in the waiting room. And no, Todd still is not conscious. His brain swelling has not reduced. There is talk they will move him to the hospital in Burleson or Fort Worth."

"Oh, dear. That doesn't sound good."

"No. By the way, Juan Estrada seems to be a dead end. He has an airtight alibi. He took the evening delivery shift around Crowley and Keene for a coworker whose wife went into labor."

"No chance he veered off the route then?"

"Nope. Dispatcher confirmed his mileage. Seems they are a stickler for that sort of thing."

Oh, well. But it made her wonder who that mysterious coffee-smelling dude had been. Perhaps if she searched the alley in the daylight, she might find something the police missed. "What did the chief say about what Keith and I found at Debi's place?"

"He thinks it might be worth investigating. That is why he's getting permission to search *The Gazette* for fingerprints and any other clues."

Rats. So much for her snooping around it. Todd must have noticed the discontented expression on her face because he stifled a chuckle, his tongue jammed into his cheek.

As the elevator dinged and the cab shuddered to a halt, another idea popped into her brain. Wanda turned to face him. "Todd, let me help. You know I can. You know I will be diligent and careful. There are only three of you at the police station."

"Four. You forget our dispatcher, Cadet Reagan Weber."

"Okay. Assign her to help me. Then you know I won't go off any deep end."

"Help you do what?" He held the door open for her to exit. Several people waited to get on.

"Sort through the files at *The Gazette* and put things back in order. After forensics have left, of course."

Todd's tone remained calm. "There is a difference between collecting forensic evidence in a criminal act and thumbing through financial records and past issues for clues as to why a reporter is missing. As far as we know the incidences may not be related. We don't have permission to look through their files anyway unless we can prove they might hold the reason for the attack."

"Then I'll ask Misty if she wants to come with us."

"Tom's wife is not an officer of the company so she cannot give you permission."

"Oh, I didn't know that." Wanda glanced down at her sack. "Well, she will appreciate some sustenance anyway."

Todd leaned back and laughed. It echoed down the hall and caused several people to stare. "I knew you had an ulterior motive."

She batted her eyelashes in a *Who, me?* expression.

He motioned her to a bench halfway down the hall. "However, I have to admit that Debi was to meet this M-person and then vanished after that. A clue to who that is may be in those files. It could lead to locating her."

"Yes, it could." Her hopes began to rise again.

Todd seemed to be half-speaking to himself. "We don't

have her laptop or phone and the computers at *The Gazette* were so damaged it may take weeks for the county's Information-Technology Department to glean anything from them."

"So, I can help, then?"

"I'll check. Wait here." Todd called the chief on his cell phone. "Hi, Chief. Listen. Here's an idea."

He strolled away, phone to his ear. Wanda couldn't hear his words but watched his body language for any signs of approval. Todd didn't reveal anything. A moment later he wandered back to her and sat down.

"Well?" Her pulse quickened. He played with her emotions like an owner dangling a string in front of a pet cat. Not that Todd had a malicious bone in his body, he didn't. But they often taunted each other in a lighthearted manner.

"The chief approved it. Reagan will meet you and two friends of your choosing at *The Gazette* tomorrow morning at nine."

"Tomorrow? Why not now. Debi has been missing over a day now."

He pumped his hand to calm her down. "We are busy with other things, Aunt Wanda, and Reagan goes off duty in an hour. I don't mean to be insensitive, but we need to allow time for a team to come and..."

"Check for fingerprints and such I get it. It's a crime scene." Irritation laced her answer, and she knew it.

He sat down next to her. "I am on patrol in an hour.

That gives us time to go interview Mary Lou about those quiz codes. What ya say?"

"You want me to come?"

"Sure. It will ease her nerves and seem less official." He motioned with his head. "Go make your deliveries. I'll wait."

Wanda skedaddled down the hall. Ten minutes later she returned to find him sitting on the same bench, his eyes glued to his cell phone. He glanced up at her. "Ready?"

She held out the grocery sack.

"What's this?"

"Four deviled eggs and four cookies. Two for each of us."

He stood and brushed his lips on her cheek. "Good. I hadn't had lunch yet. Love ya, Aunt Wanda. Let's go."

Wanda's whole body heated with maternal emotion. She loved her own kids, but Todd held a special place in her heart. Always had. She never wanted to get on his bad side. Just seemed to lean in that direction at times.

"One thing, though. I lead this investigation and ask the questions. You are there for moral support."

"Of course."

And she understood his hesitancy to get her involved. He still needed to prove himself to the chief and the community though the events of this past summer had elevated him in their eyes.

A surge of pride zipped through her as she walked side by side with him down the hallway and several people acknowledged him with a head bob or smile. Wait until she told Betty Sue and Evelyn that Todd had decided to include her in part of his investigation. What a thrill.

She resisted the urge to skip in her step.

CHAPTER TWENTY

Mary Lou answered the door, a puzzled expression across her face as she bounced her baby, Lucy, on her hip. "Hi, Todd. Wanda. What's up?"

Todd briefly explained the reason for their call. He pulled up a copy of the notebook paper with the test codes on it from his phone. "Do you know anything about this?"

She narrowed her eyes and peered at the tiny screen as she hoisted Lucy a bit higher in her grip. "Not really. Looks like a key to the answers for a multiple-choice test."

"On notebook paper? Not what a teacher would do is it?" Wanda blurted it out without thinking.

Todd shot a stern glance to Wanda.

"Well, no. It doesn't seem likely." Mary Lou eyed him and then Wanda and then him again.

"Can we come in?" Todd twirled his police hat in his hands.

Mary Lou blinked. "Oh. Of course. Sorry. It's a bit of a mess."

Wanda gave her the little old lady sweet smile. "New babies are a priority, not housekeeping. We understand."

Relief washed over Mary Lou's face. "In here." She strapped Lucy into a baby chair with a mobile dangling from it and then scrambled to clear the couch of laundry she had been folding.

Todd chose to stand, until Wanda motioned him to sit in the side chair.

Wanda perched on the edge of a couch cushion and reached into the basket of laundered baby clothes and began folding them. "Let me help you."

"Thanks." Mary Lou's eyes widened. The dear girl appeared overwhelmed with the burden of raising a new baby. Wanda's heart went out to her. How well she remembered those days.

She felt a sudden bonding of motherhood pass between them. Rapport established, she proceeded with a slight chin bob of permission from Todd who appeared to acknowledge her methodology. "We wondered if, by chance, you recognized the handwriting. Looks like a student's to me."

Mary Lou folded a onesie and nodded. "Yes, it does. My guess would be a girl's. But so many of them write the same way. It is hard to tell."

Todd leaned a bit forward in his seat. "What classes usually administer multiple-choice tests?"

"Many of them, from music theory to calculus. Though the math classes usually want you to prove your answers by showing the steps used to get there."

"Any idea why Debi would have it in her apartment?"

Mary Lou gave Todd a blank stare. "No. Why would I?"

To Wanda, she answered a bit too quickly, almost defensively. She grabbed a baby towel and folded it into thirds, then in half. "Is this how you like them, Mary Lou?"

"Sure, that's fine." Not distracted, Mary Lou returned her gaze to Todd, awaiting his answer.

He leaned forward in his seat. "Debi mentioned in her planner that she was meeting someone named M at dawn yesterday and we figured it might be about these test answers. We knew you were a teacher, and we thought, well . . . you might know something."

Lucy started to fuss. Mary Lou rose and unstrapped her from the chair. She lifted the baby onto her shoulder. "I have to feed her now. Sorry, I really don't see how I can be of help."

She began to walk to the front door.

Todd arched one eyebrow as he lifted himself from the chair. Wanda rose from the couch to follow her.

After she had opened the front door, Todd thanked her. "If you think of anything, no matter how insignificant, will you let me know?"

Some of the angst melted from her features. "Sure. We're all worried about Debi. Poor Keith must be freaking out about now."

Wanda patted Lucy on the head. Her fuzz, slowly growing into hair as soft as rabbit fur, smelled of baby shampoo. "He's holding up. I was with him earlier. I'll send him your concern."

"Thanks." She bounced the baby. "If I think of anything..."

Todd nodded as he and Wanda exited. As they walked down her sidewalk to his cruiser, he spoke under his breath. "Thoughts?"

"I don't know, Todd. She seemed a bit defensive to me."

His eyes shifted to a vee of geese flying south for the winter. Their honks, carried on the cool breeze, could be heard from the ground. "Yeah, that's my impression. There is something she is not telling us."

They both glanced back at her front stoop to see her close the door. Todd sighed and opened the passenger side for his aunt.

As Wanda edged in and clicked her seat belt, she thought she saw Mary Lou through the front curtains lift a cell phone to her ear. She wished she could be a bug on the wall and hear the conversation.

A sideway glimpse of Todd's face told her he had seen it as well. They rode in silence a few blocks, then Todd turned to her. "What's whirring in your brain?"

"That paper with the answers. It smites of cheating. Somehow, a student got the answers to a test. My guess is that it is from last semester. This year is barely into the first six weeks."

"But first six weeks tests are coming up." He turned the

wheel to pull onto Main. "It could be for a test coming up."

Wanda shook her head. "The paper is too old. A bit too wrinkled. The ink a tad faded."

"You think so, huh?" He pointed a finger at her. "And yes, I noticed the handwriting is definitely similar to the ones you and the others received on their cars. But those, by my estimation, are recently penned."

"Agreed."

"Maybe we should talk with the high school principal about this."

"Perhaps Debi already had." Wanda glanced at the clock on his dashboard. It read 4:10. "Think he is there now? It is Friday afternoon."

Todd flicked on his blinker and made a U-turn. "One way to find out." He turned the car in the direction of the high school.

A knot began to twist in Wanda's stomach. Would Principal Emerson bring them any closer to finding out what Debi had been investigating? Or had Debi stepped on his toes somehow, and that's why she was nowhere to be found?

Julie B Cosgrove

CHAPTER TWENTY-ONE

"Todd, wait a minute."

Before they entered the building, Wanda keyed in Betty Sue's number and let out a tiny sigh of relief when she answered. "Hey, Betty Sue. What do you know about the new principal at the high school?"

She punched the speaker option on the phone and held it out for Todd to listen.

"Not much. I taught in elementary levels, you know. And that was a while back."

"Yes, but you are still in the circle, aren't you? I thought perhaps you'd heard some of the teachers talking about him."

"Now Wanda, you know I don't engage in idle gossip." A stern-teacher tone hung in her response.

Todd stifled a chuckle with the back of his hand.

Wanda mimed a shush command and then spoke again. "I know, but . . .well, it might help us find out about Debi."

"How?"

"I'll explain later. I just wondered if you'd discovered anything unusual about him."

Silence lasted for a few moments on the other end. Then Betty Sue's voice returned. "I do know that his hiring was not a unanimous decision by the school board. In fact, it was a 4-3 vote. But Fred said the old principal, Ralph Blakely, needed to retire due to his health, just like Fred did a few years ago. Being the principal in an elementary school these days is a tough gig. But Fred's health has greatly improved, thank God, since he no longer is under so much stress. In fact, he looks ten years younger, doesn't he?"

"Amen." Wanda couldn't help but smile. If Fred knew Betty Sue had said that it would make his week. Wanda had long suspected he had a soft place in his heart for her. They'd both lost their spouses around the same time and had been a great comfort to each other, though Betty Sue never showed any indication of it developing into anything more. So many years later, had she changed her mind?

Todd shook his head. He cupped his hand over the cell phone and whispered to his aunt. "I know what you're thinking. Don't play matchmaker."

She plastered on her innocent, *Who, me?* expression. Eerie how that kid always seemed to be able to read her mind.

He scoffed and took his hand away in time to hear Betty Sue respond.

"Okay, I will see what I can find out."

"Great, and by the way, are you busy tomorrow

morning? I know it's Saturday, but . . ."

"No, I'm not. I'd love excuse not to dust. Why?"

"Can you meet me at nine at *The Gazette.* Todd has gotten permission from the chief for us to help Reagan, the new police cadet, sort through the mess of papers strewn all over the place."

"Seriously?" Excitement and a touch of skepticism laced her response.

Todd winked at Wanda and leaned toward her phone. "This is Todd. Yes, seriously. We could use your help if you can spare the time."

"I'll be there. I'll bring some lemonade and tuna fish sandwiches."

"Great. I'll bring the rest of the cookie batch I made for Misty Jacob."

"How is she doing?"

"Better than expected under the circumstances . . ."

Todd rolled his eyes, exited the car, and began to walk up the sidewalk to the portico of the school. He obviously was not interested in their girl talk.

"Listen, Betty Sue. I'll chat more later. See ya."

Wanda scurried out of the car and caught up with him.

When they entered the building, she sensed her nephew wanted to be the lead this time around, so she stepped back, literally as well as figuratively. She couldn't help but notice that the secretary, Amelia Smith, flipped a bit too much eyelash at him, though. She had been two years behind him in school. Wanda didn't recall them ever dating, but the girl's expression indicated to her that she wished he'd ask now. Todd seemed oblivious to her flirtations. Did that mean he was dating someone else?

Mr. Emerson appeared within a few moments and extended his hand to them both. "How may I help you?"

"We would like to ask you a few questions relating to the testing methods in this school. It may help an investigation we are conducting." Todd motioned that they should speak in private.

"Of course. Please follow me to my office." Mr. Emerson plastered on the principal-willing-to- please smile though his chin jutted authoritatively.

What was he hiding? Nervousness? Or something else?

He indicated that Todd and Wanda should sit in the brass-studded, leather chairs sitting at an angle to his executive desk. An area rug in goldenrod and emerald stripes, the school colors, covered most of the floor and water-marked sandy wallpaper hung on the walls.

He rearranged a few papers on his desk into neater stacks. "How can I be of assistance?"

Todd spent the next five minutes laying out the details. He scooted forward, laid his phone on the desk, and showed Mr. Emerson the photos of the evidence he had collected—Debi's picture, the windshield notes, the entry into her notebook, the multiple-choice answers.

Then he sat back and crossed one leg over the other. "As you can see, it appears that penmanship of the letters on this piece of notebook paper is in the same manner as the notes my aunt and a few of her friends found on their cars yesterday morning. We have not had it officially analyzed by a handwriting expert, but they appear extremely close."

The principal peered at the pair over his spectacles. "Well, yes, I can see the resemblance. But just because it is on tablet paper doesn't indicate this is from a student at my school. Many of the youth write in a similar half-cursive, half-printed style."

Todd flipped back through the pictures on his phone. "True. But these appear to be multiple-choice answers."

Mr. Emerson tented his fingers under his chin and pressed his spine into his swivel chair. "If that is what those are. That is purely speculative on your part."

Wanda bit her tongue. Oh, how she wanted to slap the smirk off his face. His smugness hit her wrong, very wrong indeed.

Todd stood his ground. He remained unruffled as his robin-egg blue eyes bore into the man's amber ones across the desk. "Did Debi interview you about this topic."

He blinked, breaking the male-to-male stare down. Tapping some more papers into place, his reply came out quieter. "Yes, as a matter of fact, she did. Right after I was hired to replace Ralph. But being so new, I had barely learned my teachers' names and what they taught."

Todd got out his notepad. "When exactly?"

The principal cleared his throat. "Let's see." He pushed his glasses back onto the bridge of his nose and maneuvered his mouse as he scanned the computer screen angled away from Wanda's and Todd's view. "Ah. Late in August last year. A Monday I believe. 3:30 p.m."

"And?"

He reverted his attention to Todd. "I told her the same thing."

"Funny it should surface again over a year later, isn't it?" Todd squared his shoulders.

The principal's cheeks became slightly ruddy as he pointed to the policeman's cell phone. "Those photos could be anything. The students in this school are not the only ones who use notebook paper for heaven's sake. But if any are somehow learning the answers to tests and passing them on to other students, rest assured, I and Vice Principal Thomas will get to the bottom of it. I related the same thing to Ms. Castro last year. In fact, she quoted me in her article that won the award."

Emerson rose from his desk as if to dismiss them, but Todd didn't budge from his seat. "A few more questions, sir."

The man huffed and returned to his chair. "Go ahead."

Todd sat with one leg balanced on his knee, writing in his pad, but his back remained straight. His body language oozed authority. He wasn't bending to this guy for any reason. "Do you have any teachers here whose names begin with an M? First or last?"

"Mary Lou Fitzgerald is on leave."

"Yes, we spoke with her. Who else?"

He reacted ever so slightly to Todd's response, then

recomposed himself. "Micky Lozano is our football coach. Mortimer Zeta teaches advanced Algebra and Calculus."

"Anyone else?" Todd eyed him for a minute.

The principal gazed at Wanda, his expression curious as if he wondered why she remained silent. Then he returned his focus to Todd again. "Loretta Morton teaches English literature, sophomore and juniors. That's it."

"And they all taught last year as well?"

The man's forehead buckled. "Um, yes. Why?"

Todd flipped his notebook shut. "Thank you for your time."

He rose and extended a hand for Wanda to get up from her chair. Then he stretched across the desk to shake the principal's hand. The principal reluctantly extended his in a limp manner as if he feared contamination.

As Todd grasped it, Wanda noticed Mr. Emerson winch, just a tad. Good for Todd. A strong grip always showed power.

They left in silence. Once Todd pushed open the glass door to exit the school business office, Wanda whispered to him. "Well done."

Todd smirked but kept his gaze straight ahead.

But from the way Mr. Emerson's attempted to dodge Todd's questions, it was hard to say what else the man might know. And did it have anything to do with Debi's disappearance?

Julie B Cosgrove

CHAPTER TWENTY-TWO

Wanda and Todd drove in silence until he pulled up to the hospital to drop her off. When she asked if he wanted to come with her, he declined.

"Thanks for the deviled eggs and cookies though. They hit the spot as a snack, but I need to report in soon, and I won't get a chance to eat again until midnight. I want to grab a bite first."

"A burger?"

He smiled. "No, I don't want to up Keith's anxiety by telling him we are nowhere close to finding Debi. Think I'll head to Sally's Salads before she closes. I could use more fiber and roughage." He rubbed his belly.

Wanda laughed. "You sound like Betty Sue."

Though she had to admit to a tiny bit of jealousy over her friend's success in losing forty pounds in ten months. Zumba, leaving her car in the garage more often in order to walk around town to do her errands, and Sally's Salads had been her modus operandi. And it had worked.

He came around and opened the cruiser door. "Let me know how things go tomorrow."

"I will, but I am sure Reagan will as well."

He wagged his head. "Yes, she's to report to me, Aunt Wanda. The chief has assigned me to this case instead of Jimmy Bob."

Wanda's mouth dropped. "Seriously? Todd that is great. Your first big one."

He blushed. "Let's hope it isn't as big as the Ferguson mansion murders. Besides, it made sense. Jimmy Bob has his hands full with daytime patrols and paperwork. And you are involved in it."

So that you can rein me in, huh? Wanda pressed her hands together in a silent clap for him anyway. Then, after he drove away, she phoned Evelyn to see if she wanted Wanda to bring her a bowl of Irish Stew from the Hook & Owl Irish Pub.

The answer came back an enthusiastic "Yes."

Wanda knew it would. Irish Stew was Evelyn's favorite dish, and the Hook & Owl made it to perfection. Ray O'Malley added some soda bread and two bowls of rhubarb crisp with sweet cream at no cost.

"Give her our best wishes and speedy recovery to the lass."

Evelyn's complexion had greatly improved in one day, except for the black eye that now had spread into shades of purple, green, and yellow.

"Did you ever figure out how you got that Ev?" Wanda

scooted through the door and headed to the kitchen with the takeout sacks.

"I guess their elbow met my head. Who knows? It all happened so fast."

Wanda called back to her as she found a bowl. "And your head? I am so glad they didn't have to shave off a lot of your hair."

"Me, too." She gingerly pressed a finger to the back where the stiches lay. "It throbs a bit."

Wanda returned with the food on a tray. "Do you hurt any place else?"

"More like stiff. This helps, though." She slurped the stew Wanda had placed on a folding table next to her recliner. "I haven't wanted to fix myself anything, so I have been snacking on Oreos, Cheerios, and yogurt."

Wanda sat on the sofa at an angle from Evelyn's chair and filled her in on what she knew so far.

"Wish I could help, but the doc said I should rest and lay low."

"And so, you should." Wanda grasped her friend's hand. "You scared the bejeebers out of me."

"I did myself, too." She grinned and then groaned. "Don't make me laugh. It hurts. Whoever said, 'Laughter is the best medicine' was wrong."

Good ol' Ev. She always found humor in any situation even if she did grouse like a grumpy bear with a toothache. Wanda admired her for that.

They chatted about other things for a few minutes.

Then Evelyn changed the subject. "I could phone those teachers that Principal Emerson mentioned and interview them. That might lead to something."

"Perhaps it could. Though I have a feeling in my bones he threw us a curve on purpose. I didn't care for the way he acted."

"Like how?"

Wanda crossed her ankles. "I don't know. Not exactly cocky, more pompous. As if we wasted his time. A king in his kingdom, and us the measly peasants he must tolerate." She sniffed and then continued her thought. "But I tell you, Todd played it well. Wouldn't let the man irk him. He knows how to handle himself. That's for sure."

Evelyn's eyes warmed. "He has turned into a fine lad. Don't blame you for being proud."

Wanda felt her cheek with the back of her hand. Warm. "Well, the secretary sure had goo-goo eyes for him. Not that he noticed." She twisted her torso toward her friend. "Why do you think that is?"

"Maybe he's picky. Or not in the mood to date just yet. Career-minded."

Wanda pulled on the knees of her slacks. "I guess. Anyway, now that he is letting me get involved in the peripherals of this investigation, I don't want to jump ahead. Let me ask him if it would be okay for you to chat with those teachers. We'll have to come up with a reason to interview them, though."

"Hmm. I will think on it. I can be discreet and elusive,

you know. Learned it from the hubs when he was in Army Intelligence."

Evelyn had been proud of her late husband's job in the military, even though his service to his country cost him his life thirty years ago. She'd never remarried.

"Let's talk in the morning. You rest."

"I will. There is a Thin Man marathon on the classic movie channel tonight. You know how I love watching the old mysteries."

Wanda did as well. "Hey, can I stay and watch one of them with you? I adore that dog, but Sophie gets jealous when she hears it barking and me laughing."

"Sure. There is plenty of rhubarb crisp for two. There is a plethora of food in the fridge here you can heat up. People have been bringing me casseroles all day. I just didn't feel like getting up to heat them up. Then doing the dishes."

Digging into a casserole sounded really good, but Wanda didn't want to deplete her friend's larder. "That is nice of you, but I think I am in the mood for a sandwich and chips. And I need to feed Sophie as well. I'll be back though. When does it start?"

"Seven. See ya then, and thanks for the stew."

Rhubarb Crisp

How to Prepare Rhubarb:

Cut from the plant stalk close to the root, cut off the leaves, and wash thoroughly. You do not have to peel rhubarb, however if the stalk is quite thick, peeling the tougher exterior may be a good idea.

The fresh rhubarb can be chopped and refrigerated or frozen for future recipes, but please discard the leaves down the disposal as they are poisonous to pets and people alike.

Ingredients

Filling:

- 6 cups diced rhubarb (or 3 cups each diced rhubarb and diced strawberries)
- 3 tablespoons all-purpose flour (increase to 1/3 cup if using strawberries, too)
- ⅔ cup sugar
- ½ teaspoon cinnamon

Topping:

- ¾ cup rolled oats
- ¾ cup brown sugar packed
- 6 tablespoons flour
- ½ teaspoon cinnamon
- 6 tablespoons butter
- ⅓ cup coconut optional

Instructions

1. Preheat oven to 375° F.
2. Toss fruit with a flour, sugar, and cinnamon in a bowl.
3. Pour into a butter-greased 9 x 13 glass or corning ware pan.
4. Prepare the crisp topping in a separate bowl, carefully blending all of the ingredients with a fork or pastry blender.
5. Sprinkle over the rhubarb mixture.
6. Bake for 35 minutes or until rhubarb is tender and topping is golden.
7. Cool 5-10 minutes before serving. Top with ice cream or sweet cream.

Julie B Cosgrove

CHAPTER TWENTY-THREE

In between commercials, the two came up with the reason for Evelyn's call. With Debi out of town, and Tom recovering, Evelyn was pitching in and doing a story on how teachers handle cheating in the classroom. She'd say the principal gave them their names, which in essence, was the truth.

Todd reluctantly agreed. But he warned Evelyn to go easy and not to rattle any cages.

The next morning, Wanda headed to *The Gazette.* Seeing the police tape around the back entrance and the droplets of blood on the stoop made her cringe. Those were from her friend's cracked head.

A slim, young officer with a coffee tone to her skin met her at the door. "Mrs. Warner?"

"You must be Reagan. It's so nice to meet you." Wanda stepped aside to allow the young woman to open the door.

As she did, Regan brought her up to date. "They moved Tom to the hospital in Burleson. He had stabilized, so they felt it safe to transport him. They're more able to deal with head trauma there and their ICU is better equipped."

"Makes sense. Harder on Misty, though."

"I know, Mrs. Warner. I remember when my grandmother had a stroke when I was ten. My mom felt torn between staying with us kids and being with her. It took her two hours to drive to the hospital and back." She shoved her hip against the door, and it opened.

In the daylight, the shambles appeared even worse. File cabinets' drawers had been yanked out and overturned, and papers were strewn everywhere. Glass from the smashed computer monitors sparkled in the sunlight filtering through the blinds. Some had been tossed against the wall like wooden blocks after a two-year-old's temper tantrum. And the monstrous printing machine? It resembled a sad, dead robotic animal from a sci-fi movie.

Wanda glanced at the now-brownish stains spread on the linoleum floor near the front side of the printer. It was cordoned off.

Reagan came up behind her. "The county forensic team did their thing yesterday, but it doesn't appear that the crime cleanup crew has been here. We should wear these in case any of the fingerprint dust is lying around." She reached for a box of disposable gloves and handed a pair to Wanda. "Let's concentrate on the filing cabinets. Maybe the labels on the drawers will give us a clue to what the contents should be."

Wanda sucked in a breath and rubbed her hands on her

jeans before taking the pair. "Right. I bet most of the papers will be in the same vicinity as the drawers. It seems as if whoever did this simply overturned them onto the floor."

Betty Sue walked in. "Oh, my. This will take a while. No wonder you need help." She introduced herself to Reagan, set her purse down, picked a pair of gloves, and immediately went to work.

Wanda came over to whisper in her ear. "We are looking for anything that may lead us to why Debi has disappeared. Anything with her name on it. Articles, notes. Whoever did this, trashed the files on purpose."

"Maybe to hide the fact they stole some of them?"

Her observation caused Reagan to tune into their conversation. "We'll find out soon enough. My guess is it was a robbery gone sour and has nothing to do with Ms. Castro's disappearance. Perhaps the thief searched for a cash box."

Wanda glanced at Betty Sue. "Perhaps . . ."

But she figured otherwise.

Julie B Cosgrove

Chapter Twenty-Four

Two hours later, they hadn't come across anything suspicious. No files seemed to be missing, just jumbled. Most of the files held subscribers' information, financial documents, or folders of advertisement layouts. Wanda did make a note of who regularly put an advertisement in the paper, though.

Of course, Tom ran one for his thrift shop. Beverly Newby ran an ad once a month for Anna's Antiques. Priscilla had a weekly ad featuring her latest brews and beans, and the Grocery Mart had a full-page ad each week showing what was on sale. Occasionally other merchants offered a sale, and Kay the florist usually put in ads around holidays.

Then she found the folder for the school advertisements. Concerts, plays, sports schedules. She flipped through them haphazardly as she sat cross-legged on the floor. Nothing jumped out at her.

She began sorting them back into the months and years

indicated on the manilla folders.

"Why wouldn't Mr. Jacobs have all of this on a flash drive or cloud or something?" Reagan popped a kink from her neck.

"Well, I have my important documents that way, but I still have paper backups. Just in case." Wanda half-twisted to view her face. "You see, we grew up in the era when computers often crashed and lost all their data. Habit, I guess. Old Mr. Pearce, who started the paper, probably initiated this system and Tom saw no reason to change it."

Betty Sue wiped a strand of curly hair from her brow. "These files I am working on go back to 1980. Kinda interesting really. Like looking over old scrapbooks."

Reagan nodded. "I get it. My grandmother has those. And photo albums, too. This year for Christmas the four of us are offering to have them all digitally reproduced for her. I just figured *The Gazette* would have already done that."

Wanda stretched her back. "Pricey endeavor, though. Perhaps too pricey for a local county newspaper. Besides, the library has microfiche and digital copies." She recalled Barbara the librarian, letting her pour over them when she hunted for information on Butch McClain's criminal past.

Betty Sue widened her eyes and gazed at Wanda. As Reagan walked away to get another upturned drawer, she scooted over and whispered in Wanda's ear. "Perhaps the incriminating evidence they sought was decades old and Debi resurfaced them during her research, similar to the Ferguson mansion incident when you helped unearth some old secrets, literally."

Wanda chuckled, then thought for a moment. "You may be right. But how can we be sure unless we can find some clue as to what she'd been working on?"

"It could be that whoever did this already has it. I think we are looking in the wrong places. She'd have everything on one of the computers." Betty Sue indicated with her head at one of the smashed in monitors that had slid against the wall. "Or her laptop and phone. Those are missing as well, right?"

Wanda nodded. She had a point. Debi was of Reagan's generation, as was Todd. Everything they did ended up in cyberspace. "And if the perp didn't know which desk she used, he would trash all of them, just in case."

"If he or she knew Tom would be at the neighborhood watch meeting, it would provide ample time to search through stuff." Betty Sue closed a folder and put it on top of the stack she'd already sorted.

Wanda sighed. "And nobody locks up around here in Scrub Oak. Tom probably just shut the backdoor on his way out to the meeting. Great." She glanced around. "Wait a minute. I count four computer monitors. Where are the CPUs?"

"What are you two ladies whispering about?" Reagan shuffled over, her thumbs jammed inside of her back pants pockets.

"Old times. These ads being back the memories." Wanda held up a folder.

Betty Sue, bless her heart, caught on to Wanda's elusiveness. She looked up at the slim woman with a smile. "I taught here for over thirty years you know."

"Did you, Mrs. Simpson? My, my. You must have stories." The cadet tilted her head and grinned at the two of them. "But we can't get caught up in the past. We still have a lot of work to do."

Wanda braced herself against one of the desks and rose onto her knees. "It's near lunchtime. Let's take a break. Betty Sue and I brought food and drinks."

Reagan's mahogany eyes sparkled. "Wow. That is so sweet of y'all. Okay. Fifteen minutes."

The ladies scrambled to get everything and laid it out on one of the desks after wiping it down with a paper napkin.

Wanda opened the plastic container of cookies. "Say, Reagan. Where are the computer units?"

"They already picked them up. Todd is at the county courthouse today helping a tech team get them up and running. That's why he wanted us to work on putting the files back in order here. That way it would be easier to search through them if need be."

Wanda sighed. That's where he was and the real reason why he agreed for her to spend time shuffling through all this paper. Did he think, like Betty Sue, someone didn't want Debi's research to reveal a past secret or crime?

No. There was no indication of that. No mention of any past scandal being the source of her reports. Wanda had read the article last night before retiring and no particular person, school, or town had been implicated. Todd didn't need to search through any of this stuff. It was simply an explanation Reagan would believe and not question.

So why waste their time?

Right. To keep her and Betty Sue busy and out of his hair. Oh, he was correct all those years ago when he jokingly signed the dictionary he'd given her.

Well, they were about to *have words* tomorrow. Bright and early.

Julie B Cosgrove

Chapter Twenty-Five

Wanda knocked on Todd's apartment door an hour before church started. He answered, hair disheveled and damp from his morning shower. "What are you doing here?"

She held up the dictionary and opened it to the inside binding. "Remember this?"

He held the door with one hand stretched against the jamb. "Yeah? So?"

"Well, we are about to have words, young man." She pushed the front door wider and ducked under his arm pit to enter his unkempt living room.

"What?" He rubbed his hair with the towel around his neck.

As hard as it was to not stare at the dried-up pizza pieces in the box on the floor or the four pair of socks balled up near the couch, and the unopened mail strewn over the coffee table, some with drink rings on the envelopes, she focused to stay on topic. "Why were you so gung-ho on

Betty and I volunteering to sort the papers back in order at *The Gazette*?"

"You volunteered to do it for Misty. I simply agreed it might be a good idea. I gather you didn't find anything?"

"No. And you knew we wouldn't. Anything of value would be on the computers you took to Cleburne." She shoved some junk off one of the cushions and sat down, praying nothing greasy seeped through her linen skirt.

His mouth made an *o* as he closed the door. "So that's what has your feathers ruffled." He crouched down in front of her and took her hands in his. "You think I diverted your attention."

"Didn't you?" She pulled her hands back and wrapped them to her chest.

He stood and went to sit on the other end of the couch, after moving a wrinkled t-shirt and his police utility belt from it.

"I thought you cleaned this place up?"

He rubbed an eyebrow. "I took a stab at it. Then all of this came up."

"Oh." She narrowed her eyes, not quite ready to forgive him.

He clasped his hands onto his knees. "Look, Aunt Wanda. I know Debi has been missing over 48 hours, and time is of the essence, but we must try everything we can. Someone trashed *The Gazette* for a reason. The answer could very well have been there shuffled amongst all those files."

She glanced at the dust-coated ceiling fan, resisting the urge to get a broom out, if he owned one. "All right. It just occurred to me that everyone in your generation keeps everything in clouds and such. So why go through papers?"

"Not everything. You found her handwritten note pad, didn't you?"

"True." Then her brain kicked in. "Todd."

He sat forward. "What? Your wheels are turning. I can tell."

"Where is the notepad?"

"In the evidence locker. Why?"

She twisted to face him. Thoughts scurried through her brain and the adrenaline in her veins began to percolate. "We watched some old mysteries Friday night. Evelyn and me. One of the detectives rubbed a pencil over a plain piece of paper in a note pad and, by the indentations, he could read what had been written on the previous page and torn out of the notebook."

Todd's eyelids enlarged. "Wait. Come to think of it, I believe there was a page missing after the last entry. Aunt Wanda you are amazing."

He jumped up and pulled her up into a hug.

She rested against him, then her eyes peeked over his shoulder and noticed the clock on his microwave. 9:42. She pulled away. "We are going to be late for church. Go finish getting ready. I'll let you drive my car, so you don't have to take the cruiser."

He nodded and dashed down the hall.

She whispered a prayer that the Holy Spirit would keep both of their minds from wandering during the sermon today. Then she clenched her fists together, resisting the urge to start tidying up, and went to wait on the stoop.

That's when it occurred to her. Todd didn't have a car of his own. His clunker died of old age while he was in Austin. Picking up a date in a police car? Not likely. And probably not protocol to use city equipment for personal reasons.

Perhaps that is why he wasn't gung-ho about taking anyone out.

She'd have to think of a way to help him get a car of his own.

Chapter Twenty-Six

By Providence alone, Pastor Bob Thomas's sermon ranked as one of his best. The choir excelled as well. Wanda left with a skip in her step and a cloak of holy warmth around her shoulders.

"Let's grab a bite to eat then head to the police station. Hook & Owl?" Todd gave her his arm.

"Todd. On Sunday?" Wanda gasped.

He laughed as he opened her car door. "They serve an amazing Irish brunch on weekends. No alcohol until after two, though. Only coffee, tea, and juice."

"I never knew." She'd have to tell Evelyn, though she doubted that Irish Stew would be served for brunch.

A line formed outside to get in. She and Todd waited twenty minutes to find a seat, and by that time she could have eaten the napkins. The buffet Ray O'Malley laid out made her ravenous. Besides fluffy scrambled or over-easy eggs there were fresh-from-the-oven soda breads, black pudding, rashers, sausages, and baked beans along with jams, jellies, and creamery butter. Sautéed mushrooms and ripe, juicy tomato slices sprinkled with parsley rounded out the menu.

A sign over the sneeze guard said it was all you can eat for $9.99. They'd need to wheel-barrow her out of there. Even so, she felt more than a few butterflies tapping the lining of her stomach, reminding her a notebook with missing pages lay in wait. "Can we get this to go?"

Todd sighed and handed her a Styrofoam container with three divisions instead of a real plate. They piled their helpings inside their take-away boxes, paid, and drove one block to the police station.

"Hey?" Reagan met them at the door.

Todd gave her a head bob and ushered Wanda inside. "Where's Jimmy Bob?"

"The Millers' cat got chased under the porch again by the Sanders' bulldog from across the street. Dug under their fence and tore across the lawn growling and barking. Terri Williams next door called it in. Said Mrs. Miller threatened to scratch someone's eyes out. Not sure she meant the dog's or the owners' eyes."

"That bulldog is a mean one." Todd hung his hat on the peg.

She laughed. "Hey, Mrs. Warner."

Wanda grinned at the young officer. "Hi, Reagan. And please. Call me Wanda."

"Aunt Wanda and I are going to go over some evidence on the Debi Castro missing persons case."

"Okay." Reagan shuffled back to her desk but called out to Wanda. "Those peanut butter chocolate chip cookies were amazing, Mrs. Warner, um Wanda. Any chance you might share the recipe?"

"I will drop it by." Wanda leaned close to the woman's ear. "Cream of tartar. That's the secret." Then she followed Todd down the hallway.

Todd motioned her into his cubicle of an office. In a minute, he returned with a cardboard accordion folder labeled "Debi Castro". He pulled out the notebook.

"Where is the baggie?"

"We tossed it after we processed it for fingerprints. Only ones found on it were yours, Keith's, and Debi's."

"Oh." She bit her lower lip as he fanned it open. Sure enough, hooked in the binding were a few shreds of paper, indicating a piece had been torn out.

Todd reached in his desk for a pencil and began to rub it across the blank page. White indentations appeared. Someone's handwriting. "Debi's scrawl for sure."

Wanda scooted her chair closer and craned to read over his arm. "M has evidence." She squinted. "Does it say, 'Meet at Big B?'"

"Looks like it to me." Todd held it up to the light.

She felt her eyes stretch wider. "That is Ben Bolton's barbeque place. Keith's dad."

Todd stretched back in his chair and tapped the pencil on the desk. "So it is. Strange."

The two stared at each other for a moment.

This was beginning to get as juicy the Big B's ribs. "Well, that means whoever M is must work there."

"But it doesn't open until eleven o'clock. Didn't the last entry state they were meeting somewhere at dawn?" He flipped back to reread it and then nodded. "Perhaps they met outside on one of the picnic tables knowing no one would be there early in the morning to disturb them."

Wanda's eyes scanned the lettering again. "People driving along Woodway would notice them. Besides, Ben gets there at dark-thirty to start smoking the meats on the outdoor pits. When I let Sophie outside on the mornings when the wind is coming from the north, I can smell it. Sophie does, too. She always barks and turns in fast circles."

Her nephew chuckled as she described the antics. Then his brow wrinkled. "If Ben saw them, why wouldn't he tell Keith?"

"Good question. Perhaps we should ask him."

Todd cocked his head. "Um, we? I don't think so." He placed a piece of copy paper over the etchings and closed the notebook. "But I do plan to talk with Ben today. I'm on duty soon." He pointed his finger at her nose. "You can go on home."

"What about getting the cruiser?"

"I'll get Jimmy Bob to take me or use his."

"I see." She picked up her to-go box. She knew her response was snarky, but he made her angry. No, more like hurt. Just when she thought he had realized her value in helping him investigate, he'd shut her down.

He must have noticed her feelings on her sleeve because Todd's facial muscles loosened into a soft smile. "Aunt Wanda. I know you want to help but there are protocols here. Let me do my job, okay? I'll let you know if and when you can help me."

"Okay." She glanced down at the scuffed floor as she stood in the door jamb to the hallway. "Tell me. When was the last time anyone mopped around here?"

Reagan's voice sounded in the background. "I'm not doing it."

Todd groaned. "No, you and your friends cannot volunteer to come in here and clean just so you can peek into the evidence closet."

Wanda pouted. He knew her all too well.

Julie B Cosgrove

CHAPTER TWENTY-SEVEN

Betty Sue answered Wanda's call on the second ring. "I know most of the kids who work at the Big B. I taught them back when they were little."

Wanda responded with a mouth half-full of black pudding, "Anyone whose name starts with an 'M'?"

"First or last?"

"Either. My guess is first, but I'm not sure."

"Hmm. Let me think."

Wanda heard her slurping. Probably Betty Sue downed some healthy smoothie while she stuffed her face with all sorts of fattening goodies from the Hook & Owl. The only thing Betty Sue might eat were the tomatoes. She stopped herself and silently apologized to God. Negative thoughts on a Sunday. Not good. Then she felt a spurring to apologize to her friend as well. With a deep sigh she mustered up the courage.

"Betty Sue. I must confess something. I really am jealous of the weight you have lost. You worked hard to lose it, and I am proud of you. I am mad at myself for not having your gumption. If I have taken it out on you, well, I'm sorry."

Her best friend sputtered. "Wanda, I am proud of you for admitting it. I know that's not an easy thing to do, and it reiterates to me how much you cherish our friendship. But I didn't do it alone. Zelma coached me. She's a great motivator. She'd do the same for you, and I'd be there for you as well."

"I'll think about it." She pushed the rest of her eggs, soda bread, and sausages aside.

"Now as far as anyone with an 'M', I honestly cannot think of anyone. Why don't we go over there for an early dinner tomorrow? We might catch them coming on duty after school."

"Great idea. I'll pick you up at 5:00. Um, you aren't walking, are you?"

She giggled. "Only if you want to trek that far. It's not more than a mile or so from my place. Actually, it probably would seem longer since we'd have to weave through neighborhoods."

"And you only live two blocks from me. I guess we could if the weather cooperates."

"Good girl." Then her voice softened. "No word on Debi at all?"

"Not that I know of."

"Too bad Bob's isn't open on Sundays. I hate to wait another whole day."

Wanda agreed. "There has to be something we can do in the meantime."

Betty Sue's voice perked up. "There is. Come over. We can go through my old yearbooks and see who still lives here. I recalled things about several kids while perusing some of the articles we sorted back into the files. Nothing too scandalous but you never know. Looking back might spark more of my grey cells."

"Be there in fifteen." Wanda shoved the rest of her brunch in the fridge and grabbed her purse. Then she put it back to hang on the peg. The early fall weather had crisped the air. Time to hoof it. She dug out her keys and covered her purse with a cardigan to make it less visible from her windowed backdoor. Then she took a bottle of spring water from the fridge.

"Bye Sophie. I'll be home before dark."

The dachshund eyed her from her doggie bed and then curled into a ball with a long sigh.

Wanda locked up and walked down her driveway to the street. The robin-egg sky held no clouds, which meant the temperatures would plummet tonight. Maybe she should have brought her sweater. She halted, then decided not to turn back. She'd be home well before dark.

A few of the leaves on the trees lining the street had changed to orange or yellow. She waved to a neighbor raking the first to fall in their front lawn. A squirrel scolded her for daring to walk on the sidewalk under its branch. The giggles of children playing in a backyard floated in the breeze. Strolling at an easy pace felt good. She should do this more often now that the temperatures didn't soar into the high nineties. If she did, her slacks might feel looser by Thanksgiving.

She arrived at Betty Sue's with a glow of adrenaline inside her, not out of breath at all. Her friend waved at her and beckoned her inside. Wanda opened the door to the delicious aroma of percolating coffee. Cups and saucers had been laid out on the counter along with sweetener packets and vanilla flavored almond milk.

"I thought we might need a Sunday afternoon pick-me-up."

Wanda had never tasted almond milk but decided to give it a try. As she started to pour a few teaspoons in her cup, she stopped. The smell of brewing coffee. What did it remind her of?

"Evelyn."

Betty Sue turned to her. "Excuse me?"

"The man who pushed her down smelled like that bitter blend at the Coffee Bean—Ugandan Supreme"

"That is weird."

"I know. I can't figure out why, though."

"You will. You always do." She gave Wanda a soft, sweet, Betty Sue smile.

Wanda smiled back. She was glad to have her as a close friend.

"Oh, I bought a bag of it from Priscilla yesterday. It's okay, but I do have to add more cinnamon to it. Smooths it out."

"Really? Hmm." She sniffed her cup. "I detect that now. But this isn't . . .?"

"No. I add cinnamon to my coffee grounds as a habit. Good for the digestion." She took the almond creamer and stirred some into hers. "Now tell me. How is Evelyn? I called but only got her voice mail. I figured she must be napping."

"Fine. The color is returning to her cheeks, but her left eye is still swollen and a rainbow of colors. Her headache is lessening, though." Wanda rinsed off her teaspoon and laid it upside down on the counter. "Mr. Everman gave Todd and I a list of the teachers whose names begin with an 'M' and Ev volunteered to contact them by phone."

"Ah. Good." Betty Sue led her to the dining room where she already had laid out the yearbooks in chronological order. "I figured I would start at the year 2000 and you begin with last year, then we can meet in the middle."

"Okay." Wanda sat down and pulled a stack of ten books toward her.

Betty Sue sat next to her. "So why are you targeting students and teachers?"

"Two reasons. The notebook paper messages, and then Keith and I found another piece of notebook paper with numbers in sequence listed down the page. Beside each was an A, B, C, or D."

"Hmm. Sounds like an answer key to a multiple-choice

quiz. They start giving those in third grade I believe. I never utilized them."

"That young, huh? Well, I think we must still target the teens. Grades mean staying on sport teams, college scholarships, and stuff like that so they are much more competitive."

"I agree. So, what are we looking for again?"

Wanda opened the 2020 book. "Debi mentioned someone named M a few times in her notes, so we assume this person either knew who passed out the answers or had stolen the answers. We think that is what she investigated for her latest article."

"Who were the teachers, do you know?"

"Let's see. Todd wrote them down, I didn't. I know one is a coach, one teaches the type of math I'd never understand in a million years, and one teaches literature."

"Ah, Micky and Mortimer. Mickey has been around for ages. Which is why the football team has been in the 3A semifinals four times in the last decade. Mortimer is nice, but his accent is very heavy so at times he is hard to understand. Still the students seem to get a lot out of his classes. I hear tell their SAT scores are ranking higher in math."

Wanda tried to keep her eyes from glazing over. She admired Betty Sue's enthusiasm for molding young minds, but it had never been her passion. Word games and word origins piqued her interest and she loved poetry. Never thought to teach it, though. Betty Sue's voice went up in pitch which drew her back to what she said.

"Oh yes, and Loretta's last name begins with an 'M'. Dedicated teacher. She's been teaching English Lit for at least fifteen years." She flipped open a more recent yearbook from the stack. "Here she is. You know her. Her husband leads the neighborhood watch team in the south quadrant."

"Of course. Ricky Morton. He has a tax accounting service in Burleson. They live on Ash cattycornered to First Baptist."

"Right. He is a deacon there, I believe. Evelyn will know. Vicki's parents live next door to them. Her fiancé stays with the Mortons on weekends when he comes down to help at the newspaper."

"Let me call Ev and ask her." Wanda grabbed her cell phone from her pants pocket. After she told Ev more about Loretta, she cupped her hand over the phone. "She says she will definitely call them after services end tonight. She doesn't want to disturb them now since many people rest or visit family on Sunday afternoons."

Betty Sue laughed. "Or snoop through old albums."

Wanda felt her cheek warm against the phone when Evelyn's voice came through loud and clear. "I heard that. Sleuthing on a Sunday. For shame, ladies." But her tone had a playfulness to it, so Wanda knew she only gibed them tongue-in-cheek since she planned to do the same thing later.

"By the way, Ev. Didn't the man who pushed you down

smell like coffee? I recall smelling something like it that night."

"Well, I guess it was a man. It could have been a woman. I mean it was dark and that person wore a dark hoodie and pants. But yes, now that you mention it. Their clothes smelled like coffee beans, not already brewed coffee. There is a difference, you know."

Betty Sue leaned closer to the cell phone. "Was he, or she, slim, tall, or what?"

Evelyn chuckled. "You sound like the police. As I told them, it all happened so quickly I didn't get a good look. More like a shadow dashing past me as I tumbled to the alleyway. Whoever knocked me down hard did so because they were in a hurry. I don't think it was maliciousness. I'd say they were medium in height and build. Slender and athletic. For some reason I imagined them to be a young adult."

"Like a student." Wanda eyed Betty Sue and tapped the yearbook.

"Yes. High school or college maybe? Hard to tell these days. Definitely under thirty."

"Thanks, Ev. Take care. Don't overdo."

She mimicked a small child with her voice. "Yes, mommy."

All three friends giggled as they said goodbye.

CHAPTER TWENTY-EIGHT

"Well, that rules out the teachers." Wanda began to cross out the names. "I don't think any of them are younger than thirty."

"Unless this M-guy Debi arranged to meet and the person you two startled in *The Gazette* are two different people."

"You mean this mysterious M is the mastermind who hired them to snoop."

"You should ask Priscilla if she hires part-time students to help out in the Coffee Bean. Or even better, if she let someone go. That means they might need a fast buck or two."

"Great thinking, Betty Sue."

"Thanks." Betty Sue turned back a few pages to begin with the student pictures from last year's book.

"I don't think she does, but maybe the delivery company who sends her the blends does." Wanda rested her chin on her hand. "Then that person wouldn't be local, right?"

"Perhaps. But they may have a local connection. All we can surmise is that the person who trashed the newspaper office is involved somehow."

"Unless." Wanda snapped her fingers. "They came to talk with Tom, found him lying there and got scared, so they dashed out just as we were entering. I wonder if Todd has considered that possibility?"

"Call him."

"No. Not tonight. Bottom line is, until Tom Jacobs is cognitive enough to describe what happened, all is speculative anyway unless we can nail down who M is and speak with him or her."

Betty Sue pushed the yearbook closer. "Then let's begin searching for a recent graduate. I wonder if Debi planned a follow up article on the pressure of schools to show high achievement scores. Maybe from the student's perspective and why so many feel compelled to cheat. It is a growing problem from what I understand."

That would make sense. "Probably something like Cheating in Scrub Oak ISD. Of course, at this point it is just conjecture."

Betty Sue frowned. "I certainly hope not. It ruffles my old schoolteacher feathers to think it may be going on here." She opened the first yearbook. "Perhaps this person she interviewed was her anonymous source so that is why she called him or her, 'M.'"

"Brilliant deduction, Betty Sue. Hand me an album."

Two hours and five yearbooks later each, the two had not progressed very far. Two Melinda's, one Marilynn, four Melissa's. All had moved away. The Melissa they knew who lived in Scrub Oak, the one who cared for injured critters, moved here from Houston three years ago. She had nothing to do with teaching.

Five girls had been named Mary but only one still resided in Scrub Oaks—Mary Lou Fitzgerald. Emma Mae Buckley, whose husband everyone called Fix-it Fin for his handyman skills around town, lived across from Frank but they were in their late forties and had moved here from Wisconsin back in the 1990s. She worked for the local attorneys, Schiller & Smith.

"*M* could stand for Emma. Maybe she overheard of a case and decided to be a whistleblower. That is what they call a company snitch, right?" Betty Sue titled her head toward the paper Wanda had written the names upon.

Wanda scrunched her forehead. "I doubt if a case of student cheating would involve an attorney, and Emma Mae wouldn't ever snitch. Besides, I believe it would have to be a teacher or another student to fit the definition."

"Well, someone doesn't want something revealed, or why would Debi use such cryptic things as calling someone by their initial?" Betty Sue drained her cup of the almond vanilla cinnamon concoction.

"Exactly. If only we knew where Debi is."

As if to answer, Wanda's cell phone rang. Todd's name flashed onto the screen.

"Hi, Aunt Wanda. I figure you will find out anyway by morning as quick as word gets around in this town. I went to investigate a disturbance on Oak Drive near Woodway. A dog barking too loudly. Turns out the pooch gave a warning. As I pulled up, a cougar dashed down the alley and across Woodway back into the fields."

"Oh, my. We rarely see one close to town."

"Yeah, well, here's the thing." He hesitated.

"What? Tell me." She felt her heart rate increase.

"Halfway into the field I found a woman's red scarf, torn by animal teeth marks. Keith has confirmed it belongs to Debi. He gave it to her as a gift last Christmas. It's her favorite color."

Wanda shuddered as if someone rubbed her arms with a frozen prickly cactus. For the first time she let her brain fully acknowledge the possibility that Debi Castro was not okay. "Thanks for letting me know Todd. I'm definitely praying for her tonight."

She told Betty Sue what Todd had said. "Coffee beans, a red scarf shredded by cougar teeth, someone named M, and notebook encryptions. What do they all mean?"

Betty Sue wrung her hands. "I wish I knew, Wanda."

"Todd says he wants me to contact the neighborhood watch captains to form a search party." Her thumbs danced over her phone sending a group text asking for anyone willing to be in the search to meet him at Big B.

"Are we going?"

Wanda's fingers hovered over the phone before hitting

the "send" prompt. "Do you want to?"

She gave off a little quiver. "No. I don't. I mean what if we were the ones to find something gruesome?"

"I agree. Let the men handle this. I for one am not a fan of cougars."

Betty Sue agreed. "Let's pray and think positive. Maybe her scarf blew off while she met with this mysterious M. A cougar picked up the scent and shredded it. Cats love to play with stringy things, right?"

"Nice thought, Betty Sue, but it was a Christmas present from Keith. She'd have chased after it. No, I am afraid something sinister has happened. I can't imagine how Keith must feel right now."

Betty Sue bowed her head and whispered a prayer for Debi, Keith, and the searchers. "And please help us find M."

"Amen," Wanda answered.

"Has anyone contacted Debi's family, Wanda?"

"I'm sure so, though Keith didn't mention doing that. I am not sure where they live now. Her father retired a few years ago. He had the General Motors dealership in Cleburne, right?"

Betty Sue glanced at her chandelier as if the crystal droplets held the answer. "As I recall, yes. My late husband bought a Buick from him once."

"So did mine. A 1990 Chevy Malibu coupe. Gold." Wanda rolled her eyes. "His baby."

"I remember that car."

"I had a hard time not being jealous of it." Wanda

laughed. "He spent hours waxing it every weekend for three years until our eldest son backed into it with the used Honda he'd saved up for working at DQ."

"Ouch."

"First time I saw a glimpse of homicide in my husband's eyes." Wanda sighed. "Let's get back to the M. If we can discover who this mystery person is, then perhaps they will have an idea as to what happened to Debi."

Wanda picked up the 2014 yearbook and began flipping through the pages. "Hey. Here is a new student in the junior class. Marguerite Humphries. It says here she wants to be a famous TV personality reporter. And get this. Her classmates voted her most likely to succeed when caffeinated."

"Oh, that is way too easy." Betty Sue snickered. "You don't think . . .?"

Wanda pressed her fingers together and put on an angelic smile. "Who knows? He does answer prayers."

Betty Sue glanced at the mantle clock that had just dinged three. "Let's ask Mary Lou Fitzgerald about her. I bet her baby is napping right now so she shouldn't mind."

Wanda wiggled in her seat as Betty Lou punched in the number. Could it sincerely be this simple? Had divine intervention moved in their lives?

Chapter Twenty-Nine

Wanda listened as Betty Sue put the call on speaker. Mary Lou's voice came through loud and clear.

"Marguerite? Yes, I remember her. Quiet girl. Kept to herself but as soon as the other girls teased her, she'd rise to the occasion. Eventually they backed off in search for other bait. You know how teenage girls can be."

Wanda and Betty Sue agreed.

"I think she had family problems. Her dream of going into TV reporting in some big city was her means of escape. It motivated her to make really good grades, especially in English."

Wanda took over the conversation. "Do you recall where she went to college and what happened to her?"

"Why, yes. She got a scholarship to Baylor. Majored in TV production and journalism. And you'd recognize her if you think about it. She is one of the weekend reporters on Channel 5 in Dallas. Goes by Margo Cummings. Her married name."

They both responded with an "Oh" at the same time. Then Wanda recalled Keith telling her one of Debi's roommates in college had been Margo. Could she be the same?

"Her mother, Isabel Humphrey, still lives at the edge of town in that little rock house. The one down the way from Big B. Used to be the foreman's house back when Ferguson Dairy owned the land."

Wanda moved her mouth closer to Betty Sue's cell phone. "Hey, Mary Lou. Wanda. Didn't Debi go to Baylor as well?"

"Yes, as a matter of fact, Wanda, she did. She met Keith there."

Betty Sue thanked her and hung up. "Well, I think we may have found out who M is."

"I agree." Wanda closed the yearbook. "Perhaps she knew about the cheating seven years ago and has been waiting for the opportunity to take revenge on the other girls at Scrub Oak High for their bullying."

Betty Sue rose to take their coffee cups into the kitchen but continued the conversation. "Wouldn't she have done that while they were in school, or soon after graduation. Why wait seven years?"

Wanda leaned on the serving bar that separated the two rooms. "Now that she's a TV reporter, she can? Or maybe she suspected it and somehow found proof later."

Betty Sue's eyes gleamed as she swung around. "Wait. Bobby Littlefield, my eldest child's next-door neighbor in

Richardson, is a cameraman for that station. Maybe we can get copies of the news reels from the past year and see if perhaps she reported on something similar in Dallas."

"Or we could just search engine it." Wanda headed for Betty Sue's spare room where she kept the computer.

Betty Sue scooted into the chair and plugged in her passcode. The monitor bloomed to life, literally. Her screen saver showed a close-up of an English garden.

"Pretty."

"Thanks. Now let's see." She typed in Margo Cumming, schools, Channel 5 DFW. Fifteen reports popped up. Glancing through them none addressed the issue of cheating.

Wanda paced. "She and Debi were contemporaries, weren't they? Let's ask Keith if this Margo is the same Margo that roomed with Debi."

Betty Sue got up and went back to the dining room. A few minutes later she returned with the retrieved yearbook. "Hmm. Debi was a year above her. A senior. But with both having an interest in journalism, they had to know each other. So, sure it could be the same Margo. I mean she went to Baylor, right?"

"Agreed. May I try something?" She mentioned for Betty Sue to let her have the computer chair. Which she did.

"I signed up for a people search program when trying to track McClain and those friends of Carl Smithers. Let's see where Margo lives."

Within a few seconds, her name appeared. After a few

more clicks to ensure Wanda was who she claimed and had authorization to the information, the address and the phone number popped up.

"Do we call?" Betty Sue's question came out in a whisper as if she thought they were verging on something illegal.

"If she is one of the weekend reporters, she's probably at the station. But we can try." Wanda clicked her nails over the dial pad. Funny they still called it that. Who dialed anymore? Touchtone phones had been out for decades. In fact, she'd had a princess style one in high school.

Margo answered on the fourth ring.

Wanda explained who she was and why they were calling.

"Debi is missing? Oh, my word. I had no idea. But why call me? Do I know you?"

"No, but when her fiancé, Keith, and I went to search her apartment for any clues as to where she may have gone, we found a notebook. In it is said she was meeting someone at dawn named M the day she disappeared."

"And you thought that was me?"

"Well, you both are in journalism and attended Baylor, so we'd hoped so."

Margo's voice became soft and sweet instead of professional and objective. "I'm so sorry, Mrs. Warner, but I haven't seen Debi since a banquet we both attended for journalists in North Texas last year. I mean we follow each other on social media, and I know she and Keith got engaged and her cat had died, but our paths took different directions after college. Hers in writing, mine in TV."

Wanda's hopes plummeted to the floor like a runaway elevator. "I see. We'd figured even if you weren't the M she was to meet she might have told you what report she had been working on. We know *The Gazette* wasn't the only paper she wrote articles for. But you see, it was trashed the night she disappeared and the owner severely injured. He is still in a coma."

"Wow. Seriously?"

Wanda nodded then remembered she was on speaker not video chat. "Um, yeah. Hardly seems a coincidence, right?"

"No, it doesn't. Oh, my. I didn't figure something like this would happen in a small town like yours."

"Neither did we. Well, I'm sorry we bothered you."

"Not at all, Mrs. Warner. Hold on a sec."

The phone went silent. She turned to Betty Sue and scrunched her eyebrows.

Betty Sue's shoulder lifted and settled as if she wondered what was happening as well.

Then Margo's voice returned. "I just contacted our news manager. He interested in sending a crew down there to do a report. Get the word out and see if anyone around the Metroplex has seen Debi. We cover most of North Texas, you know. I am to work on making that happen but as a courtesy I want to let the police and mayor know before we come so we don't impede their investigation or generosity. I'll call if and when it's a go."

"Okay. That might really help."

"One thing. Her family has been notified, right?"

"I'm not sure but my nephew is on the police force. I'll ask him and text you the answer." Wanda then thanked her and disconnected the call.

"Now what?" Betty Sue's voice creaked.

"We wait and pray that someone finds something, anything that will lead us to Debi. And that she is safe and sound."

Wanda wished her brain could convince her heart it was true.

CHAPTER THIRTY

Wanda called Todd and let him know about Margo and the news crew.

"I am not so sure that's a good idea, Aunt Wanda. We now have reason to believe Debi has been abducted. We don't want to force her kidnappers into doing something rash."

"Has somebody called with a ransom request?"

"Not yet, which I agree is unusual. But finding the scarf raises questions. She has been missing over three days now. Her credit and debit cards have not been used, her bank account has not been drained, and the last charge on her gas card was two weeks ago. No texting, social media contacting, or phone calls. As far as we can tell, her cell phone has not been in use since the Wednesday night before she disappeared so there is nothing to triangulate."

"No luck in the fields?"

"Not yet and the sun's about to set. But thanks for rallying the volunteers. The fact that we found nothing is a good sign, in a way. It may mean only Debi's clothes were ripped up, not her."

"I suppose." Wanda rubbed her left eyebrow to stave off the tension headache trying to form. "Have her parents been notified? The reporter wants to know."

"They're backpacking in Colorado out of cell phone range. The forensic crew found their itinerary in Debi's mailbox. We've left a message at the campsite's office."

An idea lit up her brain. "Could Debi have gone to meet them?"

Todd's sigh came through the phone. "Thought of that. But she'd have let Keith know."

"True. Oh, Todd. Where could she be?" She thought of her own two grown children and how distraught she'd be if one of them vanished off the face of the planet. BJ lived in Tulsa with his wife of seventeen years, Ellie. They had two boys, Ethan age twelve and Brent age nine.

Her daughter, Wesley, was on her third live-in boyfriend or significant other or whatever they call them nowadays, living in Connecticut. She'd never had any children though this one, Jeremy, had two teens by his previous marriage who visited them every other weekend. Wanda prayed for him to do the right thing by her daily, but Wesley had always been the free-spirited one who rebelled against everything her parents held dear, especially their faith.

In the background she heard some men shouting.

"What's going on?"

She heard muffled voices, one sounded like Jerry, Melissa's husband. She couldn't make out the words, but his tone sounded agitated.

"Aunt Wanda, I've got to go."

"Wait. Todd?"

He hung up. She slammed the phone onto Betty Sue's dining room table, which made her friend jolt.

"What's happened?"

Wanda grabbed her purse. "I don't know but something major from what I could tell. Come on. You're driving. No way am I walking another mile or more at dusk."

Betty Sue agreed. "It wouldn't be wise."

The two piled into her sedan and drove toward the fields on the edge of town. Slowing to twenty, they scanned the open areas until they detected flashlights and human shadows. Betty Sue pulled onto the shoulder. She and Wanda crossed the road. Betty Sue laid an old towel over the barbed wire fence and pulled it down for Wanda to step over. Then Wanda returned the favor.

They stomped through the knee-high prairie grass toward the men's voices. Through the multidirectional beams of flashlights, Wanda noticed Todd in his police Stetson. She waddled through the brush to him, calling out his name.

He pivoted and then jogged to meet her and Betty Sue.

"What are y'all doing here?"

Wanda halted and puffed to catch her breath. She noticed Betty Sue's breathing remained steady. Okay, she needed to get into better shape, starting Monday. "You, you hung up on me." She swallowed and held her hand to her chest. "What's happened?"

Jerry came up to them and put a hand on her shoulder. "We found a sleeve to a woman's sweater. Well, part of a sleeve." He ran his finger from his elbow to his wrist. "Looks as if it had been ripped away."

"By a cougar?" Betty Sue covered her mouth with her right hand.

Todd pushed the cowboy hat back off his brow. "Can't say at this point. But force had to have been used. Keith's identified it as Debi's." He pointed to a figure sitting humped over in the tall grass, head in his hands. An older man with a white butcher's apron hovered over him, his hand pressed onto Keith's shoulder. Ben, his dad.

Betty Sue whimpered.

Wanda, for once, stood with her mouth open, not knowing what to say. After several eye blinks she focused on Todd's face in the dusk. "You have to keep searching."

"But it's getting dark."

"So, you have flashlights. I'll make some calls and get coffee, water, and refreshments out here."

Todd grasped her arm. "That's a good idea. Thanks."

She smiled and began to dig out her phone. "Wait, Todd. I have another one."

"Oh?"

"Remember when you were a sophomore and the band practiced for the UIL semifinals? They were resodding the football field so old man Jenkins let y'all use his field."

"Yeah, I do now that you mention it, God rest his soul. It was part of the grounds where my apartment complex is built."

"And there were no lights. So . . .?" She waited for his memory to catch up. When it didn't, she finished her sentence. "What did the parents and band supporters do?"

He slapped his thigh. "Made a rectangle and turned on their car lights." He kissed her cheek. "Brilliant."

With a whistle he scurried toward the crowd of men. Soon, people were on their phones and a line of headlights could be seen moving up Woodway. Using flashlights, Todd. Jerry, Ben, and Keith guided the cars into formation around a parameter of two acres where the sweater sleeve had been found.

Betty Sue leaned toward her. "I hope the Ferguson heirs don't mind us tearing up their fields. They have been fallowed for decades, though."

Wanda chuckled. "Don't you remember? They belong to Aurora Stewart now. But I don't think she has a say in the matter at the moment."

Betty Sue raised an eyebrow.

And no wonder. Wanda had locked horns with the woman many times. "I didn't mean anything by that."

Ben brought out folding tables to house the drinks and snacks. Forty-seven people, from teenagers to eighty-year-olds, volunteered their time, their car's headlights, prayer, or refreshments. The county sheriff's office sent five patrolmen to assist in the search.

"Word sure gets around in small communities." Todd whistled as more headlights headed their way.

The hunt continued for another four hours until Chief Brooks called a halt a little before ten. No more evidence had been located.

The exhausted searchers agreed to meet back at eight in the morning to try again in the daylight. Everyone left in solemn silence as Keith and his father shook everyone's hand and quietly thanked them for their help. A depressive air hovered over the area as car engines revved and tires crackled on the gravel road leading back to Woodway. Like a funeral procession, the vehicles wound their way toward town, a string of red lights stretching into the distance.

Wanda and Betty Sue watched until the last one faded, hugged Keith, said goodnight to Todd, and then headed for their vehicle.

By the time Wanda got home, the clock struck eleven. Too tired for a shower and yet too grungy to crawl into her sheets, she disrobed and pulled the afghan up from the foot of the bed.

Sophie hopped up and curled near the back of her knees. Wanda buried her face in her pillow and at last let the tears flow. Poor Keith. Poor Debi.

CHAPTER THIRTY-ONE

Rapid knocking on her front door interrupted Wanda's dream, of what she couldn't recall. She sat up, rubbing her eyes as her brain registered that someone wanted inside her house. With a grumble, she slipped on her robe and padded down the hallway.

Peeking through the peephole, she saw the distorted face, mostly nose, of Frank, her backyard neighbor.

She opened the door a crack, the safety chain still hooked. "Frank? What's wrong? Why are you at my front door for heaven's sake?"

"This." He waved a piece of paper.

She snatched it, then closed the door to unlatch it. Reopening it, she motioned him inside while she flicked on the foyer light to examine what he'd handed to her. A piece of notebook paper with one word on it in an awfully familiar handwriting. It read, *Fourteen*.

"Where did you get this?"

Frank leaned against the jamb into her living room.

"Misty Jacobs. She found it under Tom's car. She had driven him to work on Thursday morning because he had a dead battery. It wasn't until the dealership brought a tow truck out this morning that she noticed it on the driveway underneath where his car had been."

"And she brought it to you?"

He shrugged. "You didn't answer your phone."

"What?" She rubbed her scalp. "I must have forgotten to charge it last night." She yawned. "Didn't get in until late."

"I know. Getting to be a habit."

Frank always knew. When the man slept, she didn't have a clue. He had commissioned himself as their neighborhood watch long before she'd formally formed it.

"Didn't answer your backdoor either. So, I pounded on the front one."

"Where is Sophie?"

She turned to listen as small claws clicked on the floorboards of her hall. The old pet had overslept as well.

"There she is. Hello, girl." He half-crouched to scratch her floppy ears.

Wanda scoffed. Some watch dog she turned out to be. Didn't hear people calling and knocking either? She used to bark loud enough to wake the dead. Maybe she was going deaf. The dog did border on eleven years. That put her well into her seventies in human years.

"Want some coffee? What time is it?" She mumbled as she shuffled toward the kitchen.

"Nine forty-five. No thanks. Have had my fill."

She squinted at the mantle clock. "Nine what? My word."

She had not slept past eight in the morning in decades. The hunt would have resumed almost two hours ago. Why hadn't Betty Sue phoned her? Or Todd? Right. Her phone had died. "Well, I need some. Follow me."

She set the piece of paper on the counter while stifling another yawn. Then her brain kicked in as the aroma of the coffee pod released its trickling brew into the *I love Dachshunds* mug Evelyn had given her for her birthday one year.

Fourteen? She picked it up and squinted to make sure she had read it correctly. "What can it mean?"

She stood on tiptoes to get down the Scrabble board. Frank rushed to help her set it on the kitchen table. As her coffee pod maker issued the last groan and hiss to announce it had completed its task, Wanda asked Frank to find the tiles that spelled out the word on the latest note. She lined them up to end on the first "n" in the word "nine".

Wanda sat down and sipped, staring at the tiles. Fourteen. Nine-fourteen. A time? Weird choice. Why not nine-fifteen or nine-ten? No, had to be something else.

An address? That made even less sense. Unless another note or two floated around Scrub Oak with a street name on it. But then what town? Could that be on yet another piece of missing paper? "Do you think there are any more of these?"

"Dunno. Could be, I guess. Can't see any rhyme or reason why those of us who got one, well . . . got one."

"Me either. At first, I thought it was because of our assistance in solving the Ferguson murders, but then why you and Priscilla? And now Tom?" She leaned her chin into her hand. "No, more and more I think they were randomly placed as Todd believes."

"Makes sense."

The two remained silent for a moment. Then she raised her eyes to Frank's face. "Does nine-fourteen mean anything to you?"

He ran a hand over his chin. "Well, I can't say that it does. Nine-eleven does of course. We all recall that day."

Wanda bounced off her chair as if someone had stuck a pin in her behind. "Of course. It's not a time, it's a date. September fourteenth. Frank, thank you." She smacked him on the cheek.

The old man blushed and stammered.

She shoved him toward the backdoor. "I have to go get dressed. Thank you, Frank, for bringing this over."

"Oh, oh, okay."

He plodded down her back steps and across her lawn to the gate that led to the alley between their homes. Halfway across, he turned back and waved, still scratching his head.

Wanda glanced at the calendar on her fridge. Today was Monday, September the thirteenth. Whoever was holding Debi had let them know they had until the fourteenth to stop a report from publishing. Yet the paper obviously could not be produced with Tom in a coma and the office and industrial printer trashed. So why had Debi not been released?

There had to be something else to keep her kidnapper from setting her free. The only thing Wanda could fathom was that Debi had decided to send the incriminating report to another source. Maybe the intruder decided to trash the original in hopes it could not be forwarded.

Of course, it could be a report she'd been working on for one of the big city papers that somehow posed a threat. One that was to go to print tomorrow. Debi's laptop was missing as well. Odds were, she had it with her at the meeting with M, which meant the perp now had it. Anything threatening on it would have been deleted by now. So again, why not let her go?

One answer. It wasn't on her laptop, so the perp searched to see if she had stored it on a computer at *The Gazette,* and then trashed the rest of the office to hide their intent. What other explanation could it be?

What had been so daunting as to cause someone to kidnap a reporter, destroy a business, and injure two people? If Wanda knew that, she'd know who had taken Debi. She could tell Todd, and he could rescue the girl.

One more day. She had one more day to find out.

She hoped that was all she'd need.

Julie B Cosgrove

CHAPTER THIRTY-TWO

Wanda, Evelyn, Betty Sue, and Hazel sat around her dining table with the notes and other items surrounding them.

"There has to be something we are missing." Wanda tapped her foot as she stood over them.

"Why September fourteenth? The paper would have been printed by then." Betty Sue scooted her chair in for a closer look.

Evelyn agreed." I looked it up. It is National Cream-filled Doughnut Day and Eat a Hoagie Day. I doubt that's any clue."

Everyone chuckled. Leave it to Evelyn to help alleviate the tension. Wanda thanked God her friend's wit had returned to its previous sharpness.

"Is there a big statewide test in the schools tomorrow? You know, one of those achievement things?" Hazel cast her eyes on each lady for an answer.

"STAAR, if they still call them that. Grades 3-12 have

to take them." Betty Sue huffed. "But not the first six weeks. At the end of the year in April to make sure they learned what we were supposed to teach."

"What about college exams? The SATs? Remember, Debi wrote an article on the pressures schools feel to produce students who will score high on them."

"That's right, Ev. I'll look it up." Wanda got out her phone and searched. "Nope, they aren't until December."

"By the way." Evelyn locked eyes with Wanda. "I called all three teachers with *M* in their name. None of them had any contact with Debi in the last few weeks, though she had interviewed Loretta Morton and Mortimer Zeta quite some time ago when writing that award-winning article."

"Why them?"

"Because they teach English and Math I assume." Betty Sue answered for Evelyn. "Those are biggies on achievement exams."

Evelyn lifted her pointing finger. "However, Loretta Morton did talk to that other fellow at the paper. Vicki's fiancé. Something about doing a follow-up to Debi's report but on a local level perhaps."

Wanda let out a long sigh. "I was so sure . . ."

Hazel's mouth scrunched to one side. "Why did we go off on the school tangent anyway?"

The other three chimed back in unison. "Notebook paper."

"Don't forget that paper Keith and I found at Debi's apartment with the answers to a quiz on it. Or so it appeared."

Hazel stood her ground. "Even so, I still use notebook paper and I haven't been in school, since . . . well, never mind."

Evelyn bobbed her head up and down as she scanned the other women's faces. "She's right, you know. And Debi used it as well, didn't she?"

Wanda conceded. "True. I have three notebooks with lined paper in my desk. Use them all the time."

"Then we have no clue as to who this M person is, do we?" Betty Sue's shoulders slumped. "I thought we were getting somewhere."

"Maybe we are." Wanda perked up. "I cannot help but think the identity of the person who trashed the newspaper office is related to Debi's whereabouts. But Todd and I went through the state database, and no one pulled up with that description except one guy in Elgin who was a delivery driver up here."

"Now we're talking." Hazel rubbed her hands together. "Who is he?"

"Someone who has a firm alibi." Wanda pouted. "He made deliveries Thursday afternoon and evening and his mileage didn't deviate from his route. Todd already spoke with his boss."

Betty Sue's face lit up. "That leaves him without an alibi early Thursday morning. Maybe he is our M and has Debi."

"Well, I guess that could be, but . . ." Wanda waggled

her hand to the left and right.

"Then who trashed the office later on?" Evelyn sighed. "And whacked me and Tom down."

Betty Sue became more animated. "What if this delivery guy paid someone else do his route in the company truck and then drove over here to search *The Gazette*?"

"How could we prove that? This isn't London. There are very few security cameras in Scrub Oak except at the ATM machines. And so many people drive up and down the alley behind the Gazette building as a short cut it would be impossible to analyze tire tracks." Wanda let out a sigh of exasperation and rose from the table. "Anyone want more iced tea?"

Both Betty Sue and Hazel said they did.

Evelyn's tone raised a decibel. "Dagnabbit. If only I'd gotten a better look at her."

Wanda halted and turned on her heel. "Her?"

"The girl who shoved me. Actually, she didn't mean to, I don't think. I believe the door whacked me down when she pushed it open so fast."

Wanda felt as if someone had just whacked her. "Since when did you determine this?"

Betty Sue and Hazel stared wide-eyed at Evelyn.

Evelyn shrugged. "I keep having this dream. Replaying it in my head. I am almost certain it was a girl. Young, mid-twenties. Athletic. Dark hair."

"In a hoodie?" Hazel's expression changed from shock to mild revulsion. "I thought only gang-bangers and druggies wore those."

Wanda laughed. "You're watching too much TV. A lot of the younger set wear them these days." She sat back down and returned her attention to Evelyn. "A girl. You're sure now?"

"I smelled coffee, but as she zipped by, I detected lavender as well. What guy wears that?"

Betty Sue spoke up. "They make laundry detergent and dryer sheets in that fragrance now."

Wanda scoffed. "True, but Evelyn is right. What guy would use it?"

They all sighed.

Then an icy sensation splashed across Wanda's face. "Ev, did you tell Todd about this?"

Her face turned the color of the rose paint on Wanda's dining room wall. "I guess I forgot."

"Arghh." Wanda buried her head in her hands. "Call him, now. Please."

Within ten minutes, Todd entered through the kitchen door and joined the four ladies at the dining table. "What is all of this?"

Wanda lifted her chin. "Trying to make sense of these notes. You know about Tom getting the word *Fourteen*, right?"

He nodded. "Misty told me."

"We got them for a reason. Whoever wrote them must have thought we'd figure them out. So why can't we?"

"Or randomly placed them on cars as he or she drove

by." He swiveled to face Evelyn. "Speaking of? What is this about you believing your assailant was a female?"

Evelyn shifted in her chair. "Well, I keep dreaming about it, Todd. And it occurred to me that the hooded figure did smell like coffee, but also something else. Lavender. And since this person—and I am not sure I'd call them an assailant since I don't think they meant to shove me to the ground—was dressed in a unisex fashion . . ." She shrugged.

"I see. It could just as well have been a woman. But Aunt Wanda, you thought it was a man. You even described him."

She suddenly felt contrite. "It was dark in that alley, Todd. I guess I just assumed it. The person had to be awfully strong to slam open the door and push Ev down like that."

He cocked an eyebrow "What's the first rule of investigation?"

Wanda cast her eyes down and picked at her thumbnail. "Never assume anything."

"Does Priscilla sell a lavender coffee by some chance?"

"Ugh, Betty Sue. That sounds gross." Wanda stuck out her tongue.

"Well, she has all sorts of flavors. Just asking." Betty Sue dug out her phone. "I'll call her."

They all listened.

Betty Sue's eyes widened. "Seriously? From Viet Nam you say? Oh, no I don't want you to special order it. Just wondered. Heard someone mention it and thought they might be mistaken. Thanks."

"Well, I never." Wanda shooed the idea away with her hand. Then she noticed Todd scribbling away in his notebook. "You're writing this down?"

He glanced at her, then continued his task. "Of course. So perhaps, Evelyn, you assumed it was a woman because you smelled lavender, just as my aunt assumed it to be a man because the perp used force."

"I guess so." Evelyn pouted.

"Which means, we cannot rule out that this person, as you say, wasn't a male. Especially if we learn there's a company who distributes and delivers lavender coffee in North Texas." Todd closed the flap on his notes.

Wanda lifted her nose. "Women delivery personnel exist too, dear nephew."

"Touché." He gave her a slight bow. "I'm going to go talk with Priscilla. See ya."

With that he left out the backdoor.

"Now what?"

Wanda slumped, and buried her head in her hands. "I have no clue, Betty Sue. And I never thought I'd say it, but I am almost ready to give up."

Her friends rose from the table and left in silence.

Julie B Cosgrove

Coffee aroma. Notebook papers with one word each on them. A trashed newspaper office. Lavender. Dark hoodie. Someone named M. The pieces had to fit. But how?

One person held the key to the answer, and he lay in a coma.

Wanda wiped her eyes and took a deep breath. She couldn't give up or give in and wouldn't give way. She cared to much about finding Debi and about hunting down the person who had injured such a kind, decent, hardworking man like Tom Jacobs. Not to mention one of her good friends.

Wanda rose, made herself a strong cup of tea, and called Misty's cell phone to ask how her husband was doing.

"He is still nonresponsive. Though he did stir in the middle of the night and say 'Debi' a few times. I guess he is really worried about her."

"Understandably."

"Yes, it is."

Wanda heard the tiredness in her voice, laced with despair. "Are you all alone?"

"No. Vicki has been here with me, but she's back in Scrub Oak with the police going over the place one more time."

"I hope our cleaning up didn't disturb anything important."

"I doubt it, or the chief wouldn't have let you in. They are going through the files now that they are back in order and also checking the alleyway for any clues, though by now . . . well it seems futile, doesn't it?"

Then she stuttered. "Oh, I . . . I didn't mean your hard work cleaning things up as futile. I greatly appreciate all you and Betty Sue and Reagan did. I don't think either Vicki or I could have faced seeing it in the state it was in."

Wanda felt a warmth in her heart ease into her throat. "It is the least we could do." She took a sip of her tea to swallow down the sensation. "Listen. Could I come sit with Tom a while this evening so you can go home and shower? Maybe get a good meal at the Woodway Grill or Hook & Owl?"

The woman answered in a shaky voice. "Would you? Just between us, I would love to get out of here for a while."

Wanda smiled, hoping her voice indicated her concern. "Of course. Shall we say six?"

When she hung up, she cast her eyes to the ceiling. "Would it be too much to ask, God, for Tom to awaken while I'm there?"

Probably so.

Wanda pushed the case to the edges of her brain so she could finish her errands, then ate a light supper at Sally's Salad Bar.

Only one other customer sat in the small bistro. They seemed engrossed in a crossword puzzle, so Wanda beckoned Sally to come take a load off before the dinner crowd arrived.

"Any word on Debi?" Sally hung her apron on the back of the chair and sat across from Wanda.

"Not a peep. And Tom is still in la-la land. I am headed over there in a while to relieve Misty."

"Good. She needs a break, I'm sure."

Wanda forked some tuna salad embedded inside a large avocado half. "Tell me. You know most of the delivery guys, don't you?"

"I guess, why?"

"Any of them gals?"

Sally snickered. "I guess maybe in the big cities. But I don't think so. Not around here. Why?"

"Just wondering. The person who knocked Evelyn down smelled of coffee and lavender. There aren't any coffee factories around here so we thought they might be a delivery driver."

Sally wiggled closer and lowered her voice. "There are quite a few gourmet distributors in the Metroplex. Priscilla uses two or three of them, I think. One of them probably carries lavender coffee. It is the rage right now."

"Seriously?" Wanda couldn't help but scrunch her nose.

Sally laughed. "Oh, yes. Artisan coffees are big. Priscilla may seem ahead of the curve, but as more and more urban families move in, the higher the demand will become. You just wait."

Wanda thanked her and finished her meal. She drove to the hospital and found the ICU nurses' station. "I'm looking for Misty Jacobs. Her husband Tom is a patient here and I volunteered to relieve her so she can go home and get a bath."

"Of course. I'll let her know you are here. Only one person can be in the ICU with a patient during visiting hours. You will have to sit in the waiting room."

"But she won't leave if I can't . . ." Wanda tried to maintain decorum. Her mother always told her honey attracts more flies than vinegar. Or something like that.

"I understand. We have to follow the rules, though." The nurse told her to wait there a minute. She returned and told her she'd spoken with Mrs. Jacobs and that she had given permission for *Aunt* Wanda to come sit with her husband.

Wanda smiled. Good for Misty, keeping a sharp wit about her. She thanked the nurse and headed down toward Room 205 and Misty walked out and waved to her.

After the changing of the guards, so to speak, Wanda settled in. As Tom slept, or whatever he did, she began to call the distributors. But none of their offices were open at night. That didn't mean their drivers didn't work then, though. She'd been to the grocery store chains in the city after dinner and waded around the stocking boys. Restaurants probably got their deliveries at night after the crowds thinned. Either that or early in the morning.

She called Ben at Big B. "Hey, it's Wanda Warner. Any word on Debi?"

"Not a peep. And here is the weird thing. Vicki has been trying to reach her fiancé, Mason since the incident. He isn't answering his phone. She told Keith that today."

Ants with icy boots crawled up Wanda's chest.

Mason's name began with an M. Could he be the mysterious person Debi had met early Thursday morning? Why?

She glanced at Tom, resting so peacefully, his chest rising and falling to the sound of the beeps of the machine that monitored his vital signs. *What do you know about this?*

"Ben, I am sure he is just swamped with his master's program. It is his first semester."

"Yeah, you're probably right. It just seems strange that both he and Debi are out of pocket at the same time."

She let the possibilities roll around in her head. "They all knew each other at Baylor, right? Vicki, Keith, Debi, and Mason?"

"That's right, they did. And Vicki and Debi were both cheerleaders in high school." Ben chuckled. "I think Keith had a crush on her even back then. Just felt she was out of his league. He was shy and awkward until he got into weightlifting in college. Built his ego as well as his physique."

"I think all the boys were that way about the pretty girls, especially cheerleaders. Todd included." Wanda remembered his dreamy face at the football games. The jog down memory lane made her smile. Then she jerked back to current time. "Wait, did you say Keith had a crush on Vicki?"

"Heaven's no. Debi."

"Ah." Wanda's brain churned like a milkshake in a blender. Debi and Mason worked side by side at *The Gazette*. Debi was a head-turner with her crystal blue eyes and long, silky mahogany hair. Nice, lean figure as well. Could have been a model.

Had more than a working relationship formed? What if they'd decided the quickest way to break Keith and Vicki's hearts would be to elope? That would explain their silence the past few days. They met early Thursday morning and drove to Vegas.

Better stop Debi before nine-fourteen report. Did the messenger mean before they got married tomorrow and reported it to their families?

If that was the case, who trashed the newspaper office Thursday night and why? And who found out about their plans and left those cryptic notes on everyone's windshield Thursday morning?

She rubbed her temple as she hung up from her

conversation with Ben. *Oh, Tom. Wake up, please.*
Something told her he held all the answers.

Julie B Cosgrove

CHAPTER THIRTY-FOUR

Tom didn't wake up.

Misty returned about nine that evening, with Vicki in tow.

Wanda greeted them in whispers in the hallway. "All is the same. He seems so peaceful."

Tears shimmered in Misty's eyes as she glanced at the half-closed door of room 205. "I know. Why did this happen? If I'd only known . . ."

Vicki reached for her mom's hand and clutched it. "Mom, Dad often worked late getting the paper to bed. You can't blame yourself."

Misty swiped under her eyes. "You're right. I want to see him now. Thanks, Wanda. I needed to get away for a bit."

Wanda hugged her and then motioned for Vicki to follow her to the waiting room.

Vicki held her arms to her waist. "What's up?"

Wanda prayed that the words would come out of her

mouth all right. "I hear that you are not able to get in touch with Mason."

Vicki chuckled, but in a nervous manner. "Small town. Word sure gets around."

"Yes, it does. Vicki, pardon me for asking, but does it seem odd that both Debi and Mason are nowhere to be found?"

A sob escaped from the young woman's mouth. She buckled into one of the chairs. "I didn't want my mind to go there. They had been working so closely at *The Gazette* over the summer. Spent so much time together. Whereas I was just there during the day answering phones." She wiped her eyes on her sleeve. "I've confronted him about it."

Wanda eased into the chair next to her. "How did he respond?"

Vicki stared out the window across the room into the darkness. "How do you think? He was angry."

"Defensive?"

She turned to Wanda. "Well, yeah. Now that you mention it. But I just took it for wounded male pride." She took a shaky breath. "He told me that if I doubted his love like that perhaps we should call off the wedding."

"I see. And of course, you backed down and convinced yourself were being paranoid."

She nodded. "Prenuptial jitters. Even so, he told me he needed space for a week or so until we both calmed down, so I didn't expect him to help out this week at the newspaper. I told Daddy he was swamped with school. I've never lied to Daddy before. Not really."

Good excuse to get away with your best friend. And you wouldn't expect a thing. Wanda hated that her mind went that direction, but it all fit way too nicely. "Maybe Mason has taken off to think about things. Lick his wounds so to speak. I am sure you'll hear from him soon."

"I hope so. He isn't answering his phone. Oh, Mrs. Warner, I love him so much." Her eyes clouded again with tears as she covered her mouth. "I texted him and told him I was sorry and would never doubt him again. With Dad's injuries I've thought of postponing the wedding because I really want him to walk me down the aisle. But, if I mention it, will Mason think I am not trusting him again and that is the real reason I want to postpone? Oh, I don't know..." She gulped a huge sob.

Wanda drew her to her chest and let the girl spill her emotions. As a widow, she knew God used tears to wash out the pain little by little. A slow cleansing, like rinsing a stain under a faucet. Thank goodness the hospital had thought to place Kleenex boxes around the waiting room.

After a few minutes, Vicki sat up, a tattered tissue wound around her fingers. "It doesn't matter, does it? I mean he isn't returning my calls. You think my initial instincts were right. They've run away together, haven't they?"

What could Wanda say? She asked the Holy Spirit to help her say things that would not pierce the girl's heart too much. Taking three long breaths she began. "It is one theory. But it doesn't explain everything, does it?"

"What do you mean?"

"Well for one thing, why trash *The Gazette*? And hurt your dad in the process? Debi disappeared a good fourteen hours earlier. And, who left notes on our cars? Did you hear about that?"

She nodded. "My dad got one. Mom told me."

"See? There has to be another explanation."

Vicki bounced her head several times as if to let that idea settle into her brain, and heart. "Yes, yes. You're right, Mrs. Warner."

"Please, it's Wanda."

A warm smiled curved on her lips. "You are a wise woman, Wanda. I can tell you deeply care for people. That's why you look into things. Not meddling at all as some people think."

Vicki caught herself and slapped her hand to her mouth.

Wanda waved it away. "I know what some people think. It's okay."

The two giggled, breaking the tension. Then they hugged.

Vicki walked Wanda down the hall to the elevator. "By the way, thank you for helping to clean up the place. It looked so different when I walked in today. Thank Mrs. Simpson as well. I will send you both a note when things calm down."

A ding indicated the elevator had arrived at their floor. Vicki held it open.

"Drive home safely. Watch for deer on the back roads, Mrs. War . . . I mean Wanda."

"Always."

Wanda waved as the doors shut and the cab descended.

As she walked to her car, she texted Todd. *New development. Call me.*

Her phone rang as she turned off 67 onto Old Scrub Oak Way. "Hey, Todd."

"Are you driving?"

"Yes. I babysat Tom at the hospital so Misty could have a breather. I'm almost home." Her dashboard clock read 9:42 p.m.

"Call me when you get there." He clicked off.

Yes, sir. Well, he was a policeman, and they were big on people not talking or texting while driving. For good reason. Still, sometimes she felt the roles had reversed. She had been left to raise and discipline him through his teens, and now he seemed to be returning the favor.

Two minutes later she pulled into her driveway. After going inside, she patted Sophie, gave her a milk bone, and called Todd back.

"Are you busy?" She heard the county sheriff's radio frequency in the background.

"No, for a Friday night all seems quiet for a change. What's up?"

"Did you know Mason is missing, too?"

"What? No. I'll be right over."

A knock sounded on her door just as the aroma of

freshly brewed coffee filled the kitchen. She greeted him with a mug then made herself one as well.

He sat at her kitchen table and stirred in some sugar and cream. "Okay. What did you find out?"

She told him of her conversation with both Misty and Vicki.

"Do you think they've eloped?"

"Possibly. But what does that have to do with trashing *The Gazette*?"

Todd shrugged. "Unless that never had anything to do with her and Mason's disappearance. A thief looking for cash is caught in the act and whacks the owner, then smashes the equipment to cover it up."

"It doesn't make sense, Todd. I mean it does, but then how is it related to the notes? And who found out about it? Someone had to in order to leave them around town."

He set his mug down. "What were the words again?"

She reached up on tiptoes and pulled down the Scrabble board then laid it on the table.

Todd chuckled. "If the chief came by, he'd think I was loafing, playing word games with my aunt while on duty."

"Well, you are . . . in a way."

He raised his gaze to her face as she seated herself across from him. "If we rearrange things a bit it could read, *Better stop Debi before nine-fourteen.* Stop her from what? Was she writing anything scandalous?"

"I thought of that but then where does the word 'report' fit in? It would be Debi's report. That is not what the word says."

"True. It just says 'Debi'."

"I gather the computers gave no clues."

"Not really. Though whoever damaged them did an excellent job. I.T. couldn't glean very much." He sighed, and Wanda realized how tired and worn he appeared. She'd forgotten they had been discussing not only a citizen but a longtime friend, who was also the fiancé of his best friend, Keith.

Todd took a long gulp of caffeine. "Keith says most of what he can recall her discussing was bits and pieces of articles she recently worked on, but most of them he thought were fluff. Below her journalistic capability. Things like school awards, 4H Club news, that sort of thing."

"Well, we are a small-town community. Until last summer, murder was not in our vocabulary."

Todd scratched the back of his neck. "True. Let's see what else we can come up with."

Wanda waited as he eyed the Scrabble board.

"Better report Debi before nine-fourteen stop?"

"What stop? As in a bus stop?" Wanda pushed a wayward lock of hair behind her ear. "Perhaps someone did discover their plans to elope. But why be so cryptic? I mean by the time we figured it out it would be a done deal."

"Agreed. Why not just tell Keith or Vicki?" He sat back and took another swallow of coffee. "Even so, I am going to check the train, plane, and bus schedules. Are you thinking they'd head to Vegas?"

"Probably. Laredo isn't safe anymore."

"Right." He drained the mug then smacked his lips. "Thanks, I needed the boost." Then he rose and grabbed his Stetson. "There could be another explanation, you know."

"That they were working on a story together that was so volatile it got them both kidnapped and *The Gazette* shut down."

He stopped, hand on the doorknob, and winked. "You're a smart lady, Aunt Wanda."

She raised her coffee cup in acknowledgement. "It fits better with the break-in than two star-crossed lovers ditching their intendeds for each other."

"Yep. Even so, I plan to cover my bases by checking out the other scenario."

"Todd, tomorrow is the fourteenth."

"I am aware of that." He glanced at her wall clock. "In two hours, as a matter of fact. I better get hustling."

She pushed her chair back and rose. "Let me check the travel schedules. You're on patrol."

"Deal. Text me if you find anything." He opened the backdoor.

"Oh, Todd. Wait. You never told me about your conversation with Priscilla."

"No, I didn't. Later."

She almost threw her coffee cup at his retreating backside. "Too bad you're too big to turn over my knee."

He chuckled and closed the door behind him.

CHAPTER THIRTY-FIVE

Wanda opened her laptop and began searching for any means of transportation that left or arrived at nine-fourteen. Considering the time zone differences, it proved to be more confusing than she'd thought it would be. Two planes left DFW for Vegas at 9:13 a.m. and 9:17 p.m. but none at 9:14. The airport was a good 90 minutes away, so if they met up at dawn, they would never make it to the terminal in time, much less go through security checks.

Amtrak left heading for Las Vegas in the early afternoon. If Debi and Mason were to meet up at seven, what would they do for six or seven hours? Fort Worth was a short forty-minute commute, an hour at most in traffic. The buses proved less likely. Why not drive it?

After an hour she gave up.

Nine-fourteen had to mean something else. The date. She did a search for important events on that date.

The Star-Spangled Banner was written. Teddy Roosevelt was inaugurated after McKinney was assassinated. The Hindenburg went down in flames.

Lovely.

In 2020, it was one of the highest dates for pandemic deaths worldwide.

Oh, great. Did anything good happen on this date?

She texted Todd at ten till eleven. *Nothing.*

A few minutes alter Todd texted back. *Bad news. Mason's car found in Woodway Lake.*

Wanda called him immediately. "What happened? Was he in it?"

"Thank goodness, no. A troller was setting up his hooks for catfish and noticed something bouncing off his flashlight. He saw what looked like a bumper and a license plate and called it in. We just pulled it out. Guess where it went in?"

"Across from Big B BBQ where Debi went to meet someone named M."

"Bingo."

"Did you find anything in the car?"

"Nothing but his journalism textbooks and a binder. It is waterlogged and the pages are hard to read. Many are deteriorated. We're assuming them to be class notes."

Wanda paced the floor for an hour trying to piece this mystery together. She recalled last year, she had four pieces left in a jigsaw puzzle and they would not fit. Then she realized the holes left in the puzzle were too large. Sure enough, two pieces had been pushed by a wet doggy nose under the edges of the area rug.

She wished Sophie would find the missing ones to this case now so the whole picture could be revealed, and the mystery solved. Not much chance.

The clock dinged twelve. Since she could not stop the yawns, Wanda decided to head for bed. Sophie had long since beaten her to it, curling up under her duvet right in the center of the bed. Wanda turned on the heat for the first time that season and lifted the dachshund off in order to crawl under the covers.

The dog grumbled with a low growl and became stiff in defiance. Talk about a new definition for the battle of the bulge. Eventually she won and Sophie padded down the hall to her bed in the kitchen.

After a toss-and-turn night, Wanda decided to get dressed and walk down to the Grocery Mart. The first whiff of Canadian air had filtered down the plains dropping the temperatures into the low fifties. Donning a cardigan sweater, she headed out and fifteen minutes later, walked in at 7:35 a.m. One other customer sat at the bistro bar, working in a crossword puzzle.

"Hi Priscilla."

The lady looked up from the whirr of her expresso latte machine in surprise. "My. Aren't you the early bird? Especially for a Tuesday."

Wanda crawled onto one of the stools. "May I have a cinnamon and vanilla latte? Oh, and a warmed slice of that zucchini-lemon bread."

"Coming right up."

Wanda glanced around the area carved out for the coffee bar and her eyes landed on the calendar. September 14. Debi had disappeared almost a week ago. But what did that have to do with anything?

No, nine-fourteen was a false lead. Not a date. Not a time. "Tell me, Priscilla. How much lavender scent is in lavender coffee?"

Priscilla set her order in front of her. "Why is everyone so interested in that lately? You, then Todd, and even Betty Sue."

Wanda eyed her from the rim of her mug. "Really? What did Todd ask you?"

She leaned over the bar top. "He asked who made it in this area and how it was delivered. I know there are some artisan distributors in Dallas that specialize in unique and exotic blends. Perhaps they deliver locally. But I order my blends online and they're shipped. Why?"

"The person who trashed the newspaper headquarters and pushed Ev down, maybe injured Tom as well, smelled like foreign coffee and lavender."

Priscilla raised up. She got out a towel and began wiping the table vigorously. The crossword puzzler rose, left a tip, and exited the area.

Wanda observed him leave. Not anyone she recognized. But Priscilla's eyes narrowed as they followed him.

"Who was that man?"

She folded the towel and wiped some more. "Not sure.

Third day he comes in at 7:05 sharp. Orders a mocha grande, does the daily crossword puzzle, and leaves at 7:40 on the dot. Weird."

"Is that what has you antsy?"

She grabbed her apron and put it back on. "No. There is something else. Something I didn't mention to Todd because I didn't think about it until later."

"What is it?"

The barista stopped and glanced around to make sure nobody was in earshot. "Okay. This may be a wild goose chase but . . ."

"What?"

"Vicki is the only one I know who regularly orders the Ugandan blends. And she loves lavender. The color and the scent."

Wanda set her coffee down. She thought back to the night at the hospital. She didn't detect lavender on Vicki then, but it had been at the end of the day. It could have worn off. "How do you know that."

"Well, her main color for the wedding is lavender and Kay told me she had ordered fresh lavender for her and the bridesmaids' bouquets. Pretty penny in October."

"I imagine."

"Then, last week Mason bought her some lavender coffee online for her birthday thinking it would please her. She hated it. He brought the bag in here to see if I might want to try it."

"When was this?"

"Um, Wednesday late, I believe. Yes, it was. Because I was about to close shop. Her birthday was Tuesday, September seventh."

It would take a very cold and cruel man to give his fiancé presents for her birthday and then elope with her best friend two days later. Wanda had only met Mason a few times. He didn't seem the type though. In fact, he seemed honest, upstanding, and kind.

She finished her breakfast and thanked Priscilla. Then she picked up a few groceries and began to stroll back to her house. Along the way she waved at a few early-rising neighbors jogging or taking their dogs for a walk.

Even in the peace of a crisp morning when her mind should be as loose as a steamed noodle it swirled like a child's top, the kind that also flashed and made a siren sound.

No wait. That was a siren sound, and with red pulsating lights. In the park.

Wanda began to sprint toward the commotion. Only three months earlier a body had been found there near the swings, a victim to a fatal shooting. Surely not again. Lord, please let it not be Debi.

Out of breath, Wanda bent and held her knees until the hitch in her side eased. Evelyn ran up to her.

"You okay?"

She eased into a standing position and winced. "Yeah. Don't jog after eating zucchini bread. What's going on?"

Her friend pointed in the direction of the park. "Don't

know. Heard the sirens and came outside. Then I saw you doubled over."

"Let's go see. I'm better now."

The two jogged up the block to where a small crowd of onlookers had gathered. The red and blue flashing lights bounced off the treetops and houses surrounding the park in the middle of town. Muffled voices and static sounded from police radios. Peering around her fellow townsfolk on tiptoe, Wanda spotted Todd's cowboy-hatted-head.

"I see Todd. This way." She and Evelyn weaved their way to the edge of the gathering just as Reagan unwound police tape in a square across the trees, cordoning off half the park. She caught Todd's attention and waved.

Todd sauntered over to her. His face appeared grim.

That is when Wanda realized the reason for the commotion. Her eyes followed two EMTs dashing for the picnic benches with their equipment.

Someone sat huddled in a disposable blanket. His profile showed a blackened eye and bloody nose. He wore a muddy, once-white T-shirt stained with blood splotches. His jeans were torn, but not in a fashionable manner. His feet were bare and caked with dirt.

A homeless person?

No. When he turned to acknowledge the emergency crew, she recognized the face, battered as it was.

Mason had been found.

Zucchini-Lemon Bread

Ingredients:

- 6 tbsp unsalted butter or margarine
- ¾ c. sugar
- 2 large eggs
- ¼ c. lemon juice
- 1 tsp vanilla extract
- 2 tbsp grated lemon zest
- 2 c. grated zucchini
- 1 ¼ cups flour
- 2 tsp baking powder
- ½ tsp baking soda
- 1 tsp ground cinnamon
- ¼ tsp allspice
- ¼ tsp salt
- I cup finely chopped walnuts

Directions:

1. Preheat oven to 350 degrees.
2. Coat a loaf pan with 1 tsp of the butter or margarine. Melt the rest and transfer to a mixing bowl. Let it sit for five minutes to slightly cool.
3. Add sugar, eggs, lemon juice and vanilla then beat with a spoon until blended.
4. Stir in lemon zest and zucchini.

5. Mix in the dry ingredients and then thoroughly blend it into the batter.

6. Fold in the walnuts.

7. Pour the batter into the prepared loaf pan and bake about an hour or until a wooden toothpick inserted in the center comes out clean.

8. Let the pan cool about 15 minutes then slide a knife around the edges of the pan to loosen the bread. Turn it out on a wire rack to cool completely, tapping the bottom of the pan gently with the knife, if necessary, to loosen it the rest of the way.

Julie B Cosgrove

CHAPTER THIRTY-SIX

"Todd. What happened? Is Mason okay?"

Todd motioned her to the side. "Aunt Wanda. Do me a favor. Ask everyone to leave. You, too, Evelyn. Thank you."

With that he walked away.

Wanda gazed at Evelyn who shrugged. Then Evelyn waved her hands and shouted in her mellow, contralto voice that never needed a megaphone. "Okay people. Let's break it up. Return home. Everything is fine. No cause for alarm."

Wanda imitated her gestures.

Slowly the small crowd dispersed, their murmurs quieting as each headed back to what they had been doing.

Wanda looked back to see the EMTs lead Mason to the emergency vehicle. At least he was ambulatory. "That's a good sign, Ev."

"Hope so. He sure doesn't look good, though."

Just then Vicki called his name, bolted out of her convertible, and ducked under the police tape. As she reached him, he glanced at her with vacant eyes, turned away, and climbed into the back of the EMS van.

Wanda shifted her attention to Evelyn who also had halted to watch the scene.

"Not exactly the way two people about to get married would be expected to greet each other, is it?"

"No, Ev. It's not. Something's happened to him. Something bad."

The van drove away, and Todd followed in the police car. Jimmy Bob stayed behind to secure the scene. He escorted a dazed Vicki to the swings and gently pressed her into one. Then he resumed his duty inside the cordoned off area.

Wanda wondered over to her. "Vicki? Are you okay?"

She raised her reddened eyes to Wanda's face and sniffled. Her eyes appeared blank, almost as if she didn't know how she should react.

Wanda crouched down to her eye level as Evelyn stood by, leaning against the bars of the swing set. "Do you know what happened?"

She shuddered and shook her head.

Wanda turned to Evelyn. "Can you run home and get her a bottle of water and some tissues?" Their houses, next to each other, sat cattycornered to the southwest edge of the park.

"Better yet, why don't we take her to yours? Her car will be safe here at the curb."

Wanda returned her attention to the shaken young

woman. "What do you say? Do you want company?"

She ran her hands up and down her arms as if a sub-zero artic blast had whipped through the park. "Mom is with Daddy. I don't know where Debi is. And Mason? Should I go to the Medical Center?"

Wanda lifted out of the swings. "Let's go to my house. Away from prying eyes. It is just over there across the street. Then we can sort this whole thing out."

Robot-like, the girl obeyed. She shuffled as if her feet had been shackled. Her breaths were short and shaky.

Wanda led her through the front door and sat her on the couch. She motioned for Evelyn to watch her before going into the kitchen to get her a cool rag and some water from the fridge dispenser.

When she returned, Vicki's face had regained a tad bit of color and her eyes seemed more focused. She accepted the water with a squeaky "Thank you".

Wanda sat next to her on the couch as Evelyn perched her lean long body on the edge of the coffee table. After a few sips of water, Vicki settled into the cushions, drawing a throw pillow to her chest.

"I don't understand any of this. First Debi. Then Daddy. Now Mason."

Wanda wrapped her arm around the girl's shoulder. "Take your time. Tell us what happened."

"I went out to my car this morning and found this." She pulled a piece of folded notebook paper from her pocket. It looked wrinkled as if it had been outside in the weather several days. "This is what you had been talking about right? Like the one Daddy got. It's one of them."

Wanda glanced at Evelyn whose eyes widened.

Vicki unfolded the paper and handed it to Wanda. There in a remarkably familiar handwriting and ink was one word, *Fake*.

"You just now found this?"

She bobbed her head and took another swallow of water. "I had a migraine on Thursday morning and stayed in bed. Then when Mom called me to tell me about Daddy, she picked me up in her car. We have been taking shifts in it back and forth since that night. I always stayed at Mom's to take care of their dog. This morning I finally came home to shower and change when I noticed something flapping on my windshield. That."

She let off a nervous, almost sinister chuckle. "I knew you and some other people in town had received these, Daddy included. I was on my way over to show you when I saw the commotion in the park, and then I spotted Mason . . ." Her voice hitched.

Vicki's face blanched again. She bore into Wanda's eyes. "Did you see him? Is he going to be all right?"

Wanda's response came off her tongue in a hoarse whisper. "I don't know. But he walked to the emergency vehicle. That's a positive thing."

The girl tugged the pillow tighter to her as if it was her childhood teddy bear. "I guess so."

"Let's find out, then." Evelyn pulled out her cell phone.

She called the Medical Center but couldn't get any information. "Darn HIPAA rules."

Vicki's lips curved ever so slightly upwards. "I know. I have been battling them with finding out info on Daddy. I know they are to protect the patient but come on. They could give out brief information, right?"

Wanda and Evelyn sighed in agreement.

"I better get over there." She scooted forward to the edge of the sofa.

"Do you want one of us to drive you?"

"No, Mrs. Warner. Um, Wanda. It's okay. I am feeling better now."

Her eyes began to shimmer again making Wanda wonder if she really was, even though her voice sounded stronger.

Vicki pointed to the unfolded paper. "Find out what this means. That's how you can help."

She rose and slipped her purse strap over her shoulder. Then she drained the glass of water and thanked the ladies for their kindness.

Wanda and Evelyn stood on the front porch and watched as the young woman walked back across to the park, got in her car, and drove off.

"Well?" Evelyn glanced at Wanda out of the corner of her eye as she saw Vicki's car go down Spruce toward 7th.

"I guess we try to piece these notes together and see if they finally make sense. Then we take them all to Todd and learn what really happened to Mason."

"If he'll tell us."

"Who? Todd? He will. We are too involved in this not to be included." Wanda tried to sound reassuring, but inside she felt anything but that. She couldn't quite make Todd out. One minute glad to have her input then the next shutting her off like a faucet.

It was time they laid their cards on the table, pooled their resources, and figured this puzzle out. Debi's very life might depend upon it.

CHAPTER THIRTY-SEVEN

"Okay, let's go over these words again. Maybe this new one will make things clearer." Wanda got down the Scabble board.

Evelyn stopped her. "Let's forget the board for a moment. Do you have any scrap paper?"

Wanda took the memo pad she kept clipped to the side of the fridge and handed it to her. Then she brought Evelyn a pen.

Evelyn handprinted each word on a separate piece, tore them off, and placed them on Wanda's kitchen table.

"Debi. Stop. Fake. Before. Report. Better. Nine. Fourteen." Evelyn tapped each one. "Eight words. Does the number eight mean anything to you?"

Wanda scoffed. "Turned sideways it makes the symbol for infinity?"

"Sure. Whatever." Evelyn began to shuffle the words around. They tried several combinations but none of them made sense in a sentence.

Wanda set her chin in her hands. "Why can we not figure this out?" She swallowed the frustration back into her stomach and took a deep cleansing breath.

"Something is missing. The key to all of this. Whoever placed these words around town must have assumed we'd have that. Trouble is we don't."

"Or we do, Ev, but haven't realized it." Wanda rose and got herself a glass of water.

Betty Sue's telltale tippity-tap-tap sounded on her kitchen door. Wanda waved her inside.

"I just heard what happened. Is Mason okay?"

Evelyn lifted one shoulder. "He walked to the ambulance so that's good. He looked horrid though. A swollen eye and bloody nose. Blood all down his T-shirt. His clothes caked with dirt as if he'd run through bramble for days."

"Poor Mason. He always looked sharp like he really cared about his appearance. Does Vicki know?"

"Yes." Wanda set her glass in the sink. "She is on the way to the Med Center now."

Betty Sue cocked her head and focused on the slips of memo paper on the table. "Fake. That's new."

"Yeah. Vicki found it on her car." Wanda motioned for her friend to sit. "She hadn't used it since Thursday, so she didn't notice it until today. She was on her way to bring it to me when she saw the commotion in the park."

"And then saw it had to do with her fiancé." Evelyn pouted. "We are trying to see if this new discovery lends any clues. So far, we are stumped."

"Maybe a fresh pair of eyes will help." Betty Sue eased into one of the chairs and studied the words. After a few moments she pushed away. "These don't form a sentence that makes sense at all. What if it isn't."

"Isn't what, Betty Sue?" Wanda stared at her friend's face, noticing her narrowed concentration.

"One sentence."

Wanda and Evelyn eyed each other and blurted out in unison, "Of course."

"What?" Betty Sue's expression reminded Wanda of a student trying to figure out a calculus problem.

"Maybe report and stop are verbs, not nouns." She tapped the table.

After several minutes of trying, the one combination that made the most sense, really didn't.

"Debi better stop. Nine-fourteen report fake. What report? And what does nine-fourteen mean?" Wanda pounded her fist against her forehead.

Evelyn shushed her with an arm pat. "Let's figure this at another angle. Why were we chosen to get the words?"

"I haven't the foggiest idea." Wanda rubbed her eyes and stood to pace. "We three, Frank, Hazel, Priscilla, Misty, and Vicki. Well, actually Tom. Misty found it on his car."

"Tom and Vicki know Debi and are associated with the newspaper. But Priscila and Frank aren't." Betty Sue's forehead wrinkles same together. "So, there is no pattern there."

"Priscilla handles coffee. Remember the lavender and coffee smelling thief. There might be some connection there." Evelyn glanced at her friends' faces.

"You, Betty Sue, and I are not involved in coffee or reporting. Neither is Hazel." She returned to the table.

Evelyn sat back. "Old Frank, besides being your neighbor, Wanda, wouldn't have anything to do with this stuff either. I mean, how could he?"

Wanda answered her. "Mason did help him clean his gutter and trim back his trees last February. They became fast friends. Frank told me Mason reminded him of his nephew who had tragically died in a car accident over a decade ago. Mason had lost his grandfather last fall, and I think Frank became his surrogate one."

"Aw, that's sweet." Betty Sue's smile warmed. "But that still doesn't explain a lot."

"No, it doesn't." Wanda lowered her eyes. "Todd thinks it was a random thing. The messenger saw cars in driveways and chose them willy-nilly."

Evelyn wrinkled her nose as if the whole thing stank. "Why? Why not just put a note on Tom's car, or Vicki's? Why split them up and place them on all of ours?"

"I haven't a clue. And it really bugs me." Wanda swallowed down the emotions again. Breaking down would not solve anything. "I am not convinced that person's actions at *The Gazette* are related to the kidnapping of Debi and Mason either. It is a coincidence. Maybe someone was looking for money and Tom interrupted them."

Betty Sue shook her head back and forth several times. "Then why trash the place and wreck the printing machine? And how much money would be there? Why not rob the hardware store or florist? Have you noticed how much roses cost now? Sheesh."

Wanda's enthusiasm hit rock bottom. And too many people's well-beings depended on her. She couldn't stay in this pit any longer.

"We need to figure this out, ladies. Debi's life depends on it. I can't get Mason's image out of my head, all beaten up and dirty. How did he escape? Did Debi help him, hoping he'd go find help?"

"I'd think so, Wanda. Surely, he would not have left her in danger and saved his own skin. That's not like Mason Clyburn." Betty Sue glanced to the floor. "Not at all."

All three friends remained silent. They stared at the kitchen table as if it would magically rearrange the words itself.

Evelyn spoke at last, her voice quieter. "We need to ask for help, gals. Divine inspiration."

Betty Sue blushed. Wanda huffed a sigh. "Exactly, Evelyn. Thanks for reminding us. Let's do that."

They joined hands and bowed their heads.

Then once again, silence filled the kitchen, except for Sophie's soft snores from her bed in the corner by the fridge.

In response, a renewed resolve effervesced inside of Wanda. An idea entered her brain from some other source than her own mind. "Betty Sue. Evelyn. Nine-fourteen.

What if it is September fourteenth, but not this year."

"I thought you looked back on important events, and nothing shed a light on it."

"I did, Evelyn. But perhaps it is not an important date to the world just to one person."

"The thief?" Betty Sue's face appeared even more blank.

"No. Debi." Wanda swiveled to face Evelyn. "When did she win that award? Wasn't it early last fall?"

Evelyn snapped her fingers. "Of course. Now I remember. Loretta Morton told me Mason was writing a surprise article celebrating the one-year anniversary. Sorry."

"It's okay. You had a huge whack on the head. At least you recalled it now." Betty Sue patted her arm.

"Yeah, I guess." She tapped into the search engine on her phone.

Wanda bit her lip and waited.

Evelyn's mouth formed an 'o'. She set the phone down and stared at Wanda.

Wanda stood up, pointing at the phone. "September fourteenth. Am I right?"

Evelyn bobbed her head.

Wanda clapped her hands together. "We did it."

Betty Sue bounced in her tennis shoes. "Call Todd. Call Todd."

CHAPTER THIRTY-EIGHT

"I know, Aunt Wanda. Mason is talking. He's told us all about it."

Wanda put him on speaker. "Is Debi all right?"

He paused. "I guess it is okay to let you know. I mean both Vicki and Misty do. Debi was never kidnapped."

"What?" Wanda felt her heart skip.

Betty Sue squeaked and placed her hand over her mouth.

Evelyn's jaw went loose.

"She kidnapped Mason. It seems he was going to write a surprise article on her . . ."

"Yes, Evelyn discovered that when she interviewed the teachers whose names started with an M."

Evelyn nodded as if Todd could see her acknowledging it.

"Oh? And you never mentioned that?"

Wanda felt her cheeks heat. "Evelyn had her brain jostled. She didn't think it important enough to remember until now. Give her a break." She winked at her neighbor.

"Okay, sure. Sorry, Evelyn. Well, it was important. In the process he discovered that Debi not only plagiarized some of the award-winning report, written by another reporter in Kansas ten years ago, she falsified some of the stats."

Evelyn picked up the piece of paper with last word clue written on it. She mouthed the word *fake*.

Wanda gave her the thumbs up sign. "So, Debi went to meet with Mason." Wanda began to formulate the scenario in her mind. "Things got ugly, I guess."

"That's right. He says she went ballistic. Said he'd publish it over her dead body. Whacked him in the nose with her laptop and knocked him down. He grabbed at her sleeve and tore it. She screamed that it was her favorite sweater and began to beat on him. They rolled around in the grass and then he must have hit his head on a rock or something. The next thing he recalls is waking up bound and gagged with his own shirt in an abandoned hunting cabin. All he had on was a T-shirt and his jeans were torn. His shoes and socks were missing, too."

Wanda's brain tried to absorb the information. She blinked and saw the same blank expressions on her friends' faces that hers must hold.

"You there, Aunt Wanda?"

She groped to find the back of the kitchen chair and eased herself into it. "Yeah. It just seems incredible. Who knew Debi would do this? I guess she dumped his car in the lake?"

"That's our guess. One way to destroy his laptop, phone, and any paper notes he might have made. Also, to probably buy some time. With his car gone, we'd assume he had left town."

Wanda clucked her tongue. "A desperate young lady. And determined. Fame meant everything to her, didn't it?"

Betty Sue and Evelyn shook their heads slowly.

"Pride corrupts. Isn't that what Pastor Bob's sermon message stated? Evidently, she left him in that cabin to starve and die."

"Or catch hypothermia. She knew the temperatures were dropping. It went from ninety to forty in five hours after that norther blew in." Wanda clucked her tongue.

"The cabin wouldn't likely be used again until hunting season in a few months. We think she's planned to take on a new identity and settle somewhere else."

"Poor Mason. How did he escape?" Betty Sue's eyes misted.

"He eventually worked his binding loose and began to walk. He believes he was in the woods of Coyote Flats. About ten miles from here. He finally found the railroad tracks and followed them back to town. In his state, dehydrated, hungry, and tired, he barely made it."

"Oh, my. Poor guy." Wanda still had a hard time comprehending it all. She glanced at Evelyn who sat there slowly waggling her head back and forth as if she, too, tried to get it to sink in.

Betty Sue began to sniffle.

Wanda got up to get her a tissue. "Todd, any idea who the thief was?"

"Debi. She stole Mason's black hoodie. He told her he'd already emailed his report to Tom. She hoped to get there and erase it before Tom came back from the neighborhood watch meeting, not realizing he'd already pulled it up on his cell phone."

Wanda snapped her fingers. "That is why he seemed preoccupied during the meeting and left early before I could catch him."

Evelyn leaned forward. "And you know that Todd, how? Is Tom awake?"

"No, unfortunately. Not yet. But Misty was able to get into his phone. His password was Vicki's birthday. She brought it to me last night on her way back to the hospital to relieve you."

"You knew and you didn't tell me?" Wanda's temper began to rise.

"I couldn't. Not yet. I had to process it as evidence. Sorry, Aunt Wanda, but part of my job is to not reveal things to the public that might hinder an investigation. You should know that."

She did. Of course. "Who planted the notes, Todd? Did Mason?"

"Yes. He had a strange inkling Debi would not react well. He drove through town, placing them on cars he knew on the way to meeting her. Just in case."

"What about the paper we found with the multiple tests answers on them?" Wanda had forgotten about them until just then.

"We don't have all the answers. Perhaps it was legit. Some kids felt pressured to cheat. It could have been something that spurred Debi to write that article, but she didn't have enough material to make it sensational, so she borrowed from other sources."

Evelyn spoke up. "Wait. Why the coffee and lavender aroma?"

"Mason had the bag in his pocket to return to Priscilla Wednesday night. Evidently some of it spilled inside it and settled in the inner seams." Todd stopped. "Look, I need to go."

"Thanks, Todd, for telling us. I love you."

His voice softened. "Love ya too, Aunt Wanda. You ladies helped us more than you know."

She clicked off her phone and stared at her friends. She rearranged the words into two sentences.

Nine-fourteen report fake. Better stop Debi.

"Well, well, well." Evelyn clicked her tongue.

Julie B Cosgrove

CHAPTER THIRTY-NINE

The next morning Todd came over for breakfast. Wanda had gotten blueberry muffins from Priscilla's along with a light blend of Columbian coffee. She'd cooked some hickory bacon strips and made cheesy-chile egg squares.

"Man, this looks great. I'm starved." He rubbed his hands as he sat down. But to Wanda, his face was drawn, and she noticed he tried several times to stifle a yawn.

"Tough day yesterday?"

"Tough night, too. Have you heard, Aunt Wanda? Tom woke up."

Her heart pounded. "No. He did?"

"Briefly. He didn't speak, but he recognized his wife and squeezed her hand. She texted Vicki and Vicki told Mason and me."

"How is Mason doing?"

Todd gave his head a small shake. "Okay. They have him on IV fluids. He is still weak. Vicki is postponing the wedding."

"Oh, no. Poor dear. Understandable. She needs her groom strong."

"And she has her heart set on her dad giving her away."

"Yes, she does." Wanda recalled how distraught Vicki had been about that. She definitely was Daddy's little girl.

They ate their breakfast in silence. Then Wanda asked as she cleared the dishes. "Any leads on where Debi is?"

Todd shook his head and lathered some butter on half of his muffin. "We have an all-points bulletin out. She'll be found. I feel sorry for her parents, though. The chief has been in contact with them. And my heart bleeds for Keith, too."

"Have you spoken with him?"

"He is devastated, naturally. His dad told him to take some time off. I think he is headed to Cancun for some deep-sea fishing. In the meantime, that news team you mentioned . . .?"

"Oh, yes. Margo Cumming's crew. Are they picking up the story?"

"It will be on the evening news. So be sure to watch. You might even see my ugly face." He chuckled.

"Todd. Shame on you. You are a handsome man. And the young ladies of this town are noticing it. Just in case you hadn't noticed them noticing."

He tried to hide his embarrassment by reaching down to pet Sophie and sneak her the last small piece of bacon. "Well, I am going to get some shut eye. Thanks again for breakfast. See you Thursday for Scrabble?"

She kissed his cheek. "It's a date."

He laughed. "First one I've had in a while."

I know. Wanda wondered what she could do to change that fact.

Wanda called Betty Sue and Evelyn to fill them in on all Todd had told her. Then she phoned Hazel, Frank, and Priscilla inviting them to her house for a potluck and to watch the six-o'clock evening news out of Dallas. As the day progressed, though, more and more of the town heard about it and wanted to watch, so Pastor Bob opened the fellowship hall and streamed the show onto the projector screen for those who didn't subscribe to cable.

Over one hundred people showed up, most with food in hand to contribute to the feast. The chief let Todd have the evening off. Todd's face paled when he walked in to ear-piercing cheers and clapping.

"Aunt Wanda. So many people. How in the world?"

She shrugged. "You know Scrub Oak. Word gets around."

People piled goodies on paper plates and sat at long tables chatting and having a great time. That was what Wanda loved about her town. Spontaneous gatherings such as this. It warmed her heart to know so many citizens cared about their local hero.

Everyone applauded and whistled when they saw Todd being interviewed. He blushed like a schoolboy when the girl he'd crushed on glanced his way. Wanda also noticed his chest swell. Her nephew, once the quiet, lanky kid of divorced parents who'd abandoned him to find their own new lives, had come into his own.

Wanda's own pride elevated to a new height.

Cheesy Chile Egg Squares

Ingredients:

- 6 eggs whipped to a soft yellow color
- 32 oz of shredded cheddar cheese
- 1 small can of chopped green chiles, drained
- 1 12 oz can of evaporated milk
- ¼ tsp salt

Directions:

1. Preheat oven to 375 degrees
2. Grease a glass casserole pan.
3. Pour in the eggs, cheese, and chiles.
4. Pour the evaporated milk over the rest.
5. Bake for 25 minutes or until lightly toasted.
6. Cool for 20 minutes then slice into 2-inch squares.

Serving size: 2-3 squares

Reheat each serving in the microwave for 20-30 seconds.

Top with salsa or Pico de Gallo if desired.

CHAPTER FORTY

Two days later, Tom became lucid enough to speak and eat. He was transferred to a rehabilitation hospital in Fort Worth that specialized in brain trauma recovery.

Wanda talked to her pastor at Holy Hill and Evelyn spoke to hers at First Baptist. Both churches in town took up a collection for Misty to stay in a suite hotel nearby so she didn't have to commute back and forth. Wanda recalled the days when her late hubby had to make that trek to find work. Even though it was about an hour away, it often meant sitting in bumper-to-bumper traffic.

Wanda's phone rang. "Hi, it's Vicki. I wanted you to know that Mason is being discharged today."

"I am so very glad you called to tell me. How's your dad?"

"He is progressing though it will be several months before he is able to come home. So, the wedding is definitely on hold. Mason is disappointed but under the circumstances, he understands."

"That is a shame, but I am glad Mason is on the mend and Tom will be all right. How are you holding up?"

Her voice became a bit more upbeat. "Well, I am a lady of leisure for the moment. But there is great news. The Texas Association of Reporters is having a fund raiser in Dallas to help get *The Gazette* operational again. Mason and I will be running things until Daddy is up to returning. The doctors believe that won't be until after the holidays, though. In the meantime, Barbara Mills at the library is letting me use the computers there. We are sending out the paper via email and posting it on a website that Mason is designing while he recuperates."

Wanda let her know how proud she was of both of them and thanked her for the call. But something else began to brew in her mind.

She called Betty Sue and Evelyn and asked them to meet her at the Hook & Owl for dinner. It was Irish Stew night, so Evelyn was certainly up for it. There, over good food, the three of them cooked up a secret plan.

The next morning, Betty Sue and Wanda drove to Fort Worth to meet with Misty and let her in on it. She began to cry. "I think it is a marvelous idea. Tom will be so pleased."

Plan in motion, Wanda called Kay, the florist. She agreed to donate the flowers to the cause. Priscilla and Sally agreed to provide the food and drinks. The Grocery Mart donated the paper goods and plastic utensils.

Two weeks later, Misty phoned Vicki and told her to head to Fort Worth, and to bring Mason with her.

A blanched-faced daughter entered her father's hospital room to find it decorated in lavender and white streamers from which hung doves and silver bells. Pastor Bob stood there, Bible clutched in his hands.

Wanda handed her a bouquet of baby's breath and fresh lavender, courtesy of Kay's Flowers. Todd stepped forward as the best man. Her old college roommate, Rebecca Epson, who had been the head cheerleader in high school during Todd's senior year, stood in to be her maid of honor.

Tom Jacobs sat in a wheelchair dressed in a tux. Misty wore a long, velvet dress in dark purple.

Vicki squealed with joy, her hands to her face.

Mason winked and pulled out a black velvet jewelry box containing two gold wedding bands.

"Mason, you knew about this?" Vicki's eyes shimmered, reflecting the hospital room's fluorescent lights.

Rebecca whispered into her ear. "Your gown is in the bathroom. I'd go change if I were you."

Todd held his and Mason's tuxes in a garment bag. The two went down the hall to the men's room to get ready.

Fifteen minutes later, Vicki Jacobs became Mrs. Mason Clyburn, after her father gave her away.

Betty Sue and Evelyn attended along with Priscilla, Sally, and a few others. Keith, sporting a new tan, came as well, and when his friend kissed his bride, Keith clapped the loudest.

After the ceremony, Vicki asked Wanda how she

arranged it all. Wanda hugged her. "Lots of people pitched in. You know how word gets around."

A small reception was held in the rehabilitation recreation room after the ceremony. The bride and groom danced as people watched, and Wanda noticed Tom Jacob's smile reach his cheekbones. A great thing to witness.

Misty lived up to her name, dabbing her eyes with tissues. As mother of the bride, she had every right to do so. Wanda squeezed her hand. Her eyes became sort of misty as well.

Then Wanda turned to view something else that warmed her heart. Todd and Rebecca deep in conversation. Rebecca's expression as she gazed up into Todd's face was unmistakably one of interest and admiration. She brushed his arm with her hand and his grin widened.

Perhaps in a year or so there would be another wedding in Scrub Oak. Wanda sent up a small prayer, hoping God didn't mind her making the suggestion.

Not that she would ever meddle ...

Acknowledgements

First of all, I cannot thank my publisher, Marji Lane of Write Integrity Press, enough for believing in this series and contracting me to write them. Her cover designs are amazing and her editorial staff so thorough and knowledgeable. I am truly blessed to be one of her authors. And to Shirley Crowder for taking the time to edit it. Also, I want to thank Larry and Barbara Mills for their willingness to read the draft and catch typos.

I want to thank my friends who have allowed me to honor them by using their names in these books. It is one small way I can show them how much I appreciate their support, prayers, and enthusiasm.

And I want to thank my son, James, for coming up with the ultimate twist at the end with Debi. I keep telling him he should be writing as well.

And to you, dear reader, for buying the book and taking the time to read it. It means a lot to me. I hope you have enjoyed the story as you followed this mystery.

May God's love never be a mystery to you. He is always there, and He cares.

About the Author

Julie B Cosgrove developed a passion for words at a young age. She began with word search puzzles. Then she solved the word games in the daily newspapers. She and her mother shared many fun hours playing Scrabble and Hang Man.

Then, another passion developed—whodunnits. She loved the Charlie Chan, Sherlock Holmes, and Hercule Poirot movies that played on Saturday afternoons on TV. Nancy Drew and the romantic mystery novels of the late Mary Stewart and Victoria Holt kept her eyes dancing over the pages through her school years.

Later in her adult life, her passion for Christ spurred her to write faith-based fiction and devotionals for several publications, which she has been doing since 2009. Her blog, *Where Did You Find God Today?* now has readers in over fifty countries.

But her passion remains mystery, the cozier the better. Now, she has mysteries stacked up on her watchlist on

Britbox and a long list of cozies on her e-reader's to-be-read list. She loves to write them as well.

Her first cozy, *Dumpster Dicing*, won Best Mystery by the Texas Association of Authors in 2017. She has three series published—The Bunco Biddies Mysteries, The Relatively Seeking Mysteries, and this new series, the Wordplay Mysteries.

You can find all of her fiction and nonfiction books as well as her blog's link on her website, www.juliebcosgrove.com.

Suspense & Mystery from Pursued Books

Thank you
for reading our books!

Look for other books
published by

P

Pursued Books
an imprint of

W

Write Integrity Press
www.WriteIntegrity.com